JACK AND MACK IN THE QUEST FOR THE SWORD OF FIRE

JOHN R. BECK

authorHOUSE®

AuthorHouse™
1663 Liberty Drive
Bloomington, IN 47403
www.authorhouse.com
Phone: 1 (800) 839-8640

Cover Illustrator: Santiago Martinez
Editor: Rebecca Straple

www.talesofeden.com
Kalamazoo, MI 49009

Published by AuthorHouse 04/15/2019

ISBN: 978-1-7283-0747-3 (sc)
ISBN: 978-1-7283-0746-6 (e)

Library of Congress Control Number: 2019904118

Print information available on the last page.

This book is printed on acid-free paper.

Contents

Author's Apology vii
Prologue ix

1. Jack's Tale Begins 1
2. Mack's Tale Begins 10
3. Jack's Apology 18
4. Mack's Elephant 27
5. Jack's Fall 36
6. Ben's Courage 45
7. Mack's Apple 55
8. Jack Sets Sail 64
9. Mack's Bumpy Ride 74
10. Jack's Steps of Sorrow 83
11. Jack and Mack Collide 92
12. Mack's Anger 101
13. Jack's Faith 109
14. After the Fire 117

Epilogue 125
People 126
Places 128
Postscript 129

Author's Apology

Dear Reader,

This book contains two coming-of-age quests featuring twelve-year-old boys. One is a Sethite named Jack and the other is a Cainite named Mack. They may even meet.

Consider this book an example of apologetics fiction: imagination anchored by actual events from the Holy Bible. Check out www.talesofeden.com for educational resources.

Several people deserve special thanks for helping me finish this book. Tiffany Blum and Mr. Horrock's fifth-grade class critiqued my plot and dialogue. Santiago Martinez illustrated the cover. My family put up with my endless rewrites. But most of all, I thank the Lord for the work that He has done, is doing, and will do in my life.

Now, in my book, you may find a sword, but you won't find any sorcery. If the thought of riding a dinosaur thrills you then read on and see where that T-rex just might take you!

- John R. Beck, 2019

Prologue

"The LORD God made garments of skin for Adam and his wife and clothed them. And the LORD God said, 'The man has now become like one of Us, knowing good and evil. He must not be allowed to reach out his hand and take also from the tree of life and eat, and live forever.'

So the LORD God banished him from the Garden of Eden to work the ground from which he had been taken. After He drove the man out, He placed on the east side of the Garden of Eden cherubim and a flaming sword flashing back and forth to guard the way to the tree of life."

- Genesis 3:21-24

Chapter 1
Jack's Tale Begins

Never feed your dinosaur something that smells like you or they may munch on you instead of your enemy. That was why a nine-foot-tall giant named Rog dumped stinky volcanic ash all over his bulky orange and black armor. He also covered his head and hands with green war paint just to look scary. Then Rog lumbered down a tunnel into a massive cavern inside a dormant volcano. The volcano, called Neth, was located deep in the harsh Unknown Lands.

Once inside the cavern, Rog mounted his carnotaur. It reared up and roared! At Rog's command two thousand warriors mounted their carnotaurs. These eight-foot-tall, supernaturally sinister giants were called the Nethog. Rog then promised Emperor Og that he would conquer the Known Lands to avenge their banishment. But Rog also had a secret plan and needed the Sword of Fire to do it.

* * *

Jack, a firstborn Sethite, could not sleep. He tossed and turned in the early hours of his twelfth birthday. Today began Jack's pilgrimage with his Great-grandpa Eli to see the Sword of Fire. The Sword of Fire guarded the entrance to the Garden of Eden which had been the first home of Adam and Eve. Jack had waited his whole life to come of age and dawn still seemed so far off. He rolled left. He rolled right. Finally, he sat up in bed very wide awake.

Jack was a strong, stocky kid with short blond hair. He was already wearing his favorite brown pants and blue shirt so he could roll out of bed at a moment's notice. But at this moment he had nowhere to go. Looking out of his second-story window, he could see the courtyard below and just make out the Village of Noll down the road. An early morning mist covered the whole valley. He lived in a fortress on the frontier of the western

Lands of Neer. All sorts of wild dinosaurs roamed everywhere nearby. But it was oddly quiet at the moment. Too quiet!

Jack grabbed his slingshot. He didn't always need it but he took it everywhere. He headed for the tower in the center of the courtyard where his dad, George, usually prayed. Jack understood his dad called upon the Lord, but Jack sometimes wondered if God ever called back. Sure, Adam and Eve had walked and talked with God in the Garden of Eden. But that had been over four hundred years ago, and few people believed their Tales of Eden these days.

While walking across the courtyard Jack heard the dreaded sound of leathery wings flapping. Three hungry and hostile pterodactyls flew straight at him. He killed one of them with his slingshot and ducked under the second one. Then he rolled over and nailed that pterodactyl too. But now he was out of ammo! The third pterodactyl dove at him. This was going to hurt.

Suddenly a stone whistled through the air, killing the vicious thing instantly. Jack looked up and saw his dad slowly lowering his lethal sling.

"Why did you move out here?!" Jack called out. But he already knew the answer.

"God commanded us to fill the earth…to

conquer and care for it," said George. "So, I moved down here to the frontier with my brothers. We built this rope bridge to cross the Deep Drop. Then I met and married your mother. She is so beautiful."

"That's gross, Dad!" said Jack as he leapt up the steps two at a time. When he reached the top he asked, "When will Great-grandpa Eli get here?"

"Old Eli does what he wants in the time that he needs," said his dad with a shrug. "Did you know your Great-grandpa Eli took your Grandpa Daniel to see the Sword of Fire? Then Eli took me to see it when I turned twelve."

"Dad!"

"Ok, ok, no more family history," laughed George. He knelt to pray with the rising of the sun. When Jack didn't join him in prayer George asked, "Would your mother like your help making breakfast while you wait?"

"...Yeah," said Jack. He walked slowly down the steps, thinking that his Dad's questions always seemed more like commands.

* * *

Jack's mom, Geneva, missed yet another sunrise. Instead, she worked alongside her servants, making breakfast in the kitchen. But her back ached as her unborn child kept kicking.

Jack walked in, plopped down in the middle of everything, and said, "Morning, Mom."

"Good morning, Jack."

"When will Great-grandpa Eli get here?"

"I don't know. I hope soon," said his mom.

"Me too!" Jack stood up, drew out an imaginary sword, and started waving it around. He asked, "Do you think the sword ever catches the Garden of Eden on fire?"

"I doubt it. Cherubim guard it all day and night," replied his mom, rubbing her sore back. "Could you please wake up Josh and bring me Holly?"

"Aww…ok," mumbled Jack as he grumbled his way to the bed-chambers of his sleeping siblings. Jack pushed his brother out of bed as a joke. Then he hurried to Holly's room. She was crying, as usual. He waited as their new nanny, Sarah, changed Holly's diaper. Then Jack made a funny face and Holly started giggling as he carried her to their mom.

* * *

Jack and Josh argued at breakfast about whether or not Cainites ate meat until Sarah told them to be quiet. Jack glared at his brother and then looked around the dining hall at the hundreds of people eating fruits and vegetables. They had all come to celebrate his coming of age. He had no idea how many relatives he had. A mural of their family tree on the wall in the hall had the First Parents at the top. But he never looked at it.

Suddenly the hall's large doors burst open. Jack's Grandpa Daniel carried in his seven-foot-long white staff made of hardened gopher wood. He banged it on a table to hush the crowd. Daniel governed his Lands of Neer with a just hand, so everyone stopped talking. Then he announced that his father, Eli, had disappeared!

Jack watched his dad quickly leave the hall with Grandpa Daniel. They were followed by Daniel's brave Blue Buccaneers, who protected the Lands of Neer. Jack and Josh decided to join the search. They raced down into the cellars, through a maze of storage tunnels, and up into the stables. They found their dad amid all the hustle and bustle and asked if they could go.

"Sorry, boys, not this time," George said. He worried about what could possibly stop Eli from doing anything! After all, old Eli was a first-generation descendent of the First Parents. He was a mighty man of great renown who reigned and ruled over all the Known Lands.

"Let's go," said Daniel. "My father must be found today!" Guards opened the gates and the search party headed out in a cloud of dust.

* * *

Jack and Josh did not want to help their mom clean up the dining hall, so they went cliff jumping in a tributary of the Pishon River. After diving for a while Josh began to tire. Jack slyly asked Josh to jump just one more time. Then, as a joke, Jack pushed past Josh and jumped off first. But Josh slipped and fell backwards off the cliff. When Josh did not come up for air, Jack quickly dove underwater looking for him. Jack found Josh floating unconscious and dragged him onto the shore in the tall grass.

Josh spluttered and coughed. A nasty gash bled on his forehead. Jack tried helping Josh sit up but Josh just fell over. Jack decided to carry his brother back home. As Jack lifted Josh, they came face to face with the pointed end of a spear! It had a red tip with a black shaft. A bald man with a black goatee held it ready for action.

"Far from home, boys?!" asked Karl the Cainite, waving his spear at them.

Jack said nothing. He just shook with fear at the sight of the fierce Red Thorn Ranger from the fearsome Lands of Noor.

"Jack! Josh!" called out voices not too far back up the trail toward home.

"I would make you my slaves," said Karl, "but I don't have enough time to do it." Then Karl disappeared into the brush just as a few Blue Buccaneers appeared.

Most of the soldiers rushed past Jack and Josh, searching for the mysterious Red Thorn Ranger. But Ben, the new Captain of the Guard, stopped. He wore blue and white Sethite armor with the symbol of a white dove on his chest and a long whip fastened at his waist. He scooped up both boys and ran them back to safety.

* * *

Jack sat waiting for his mom outside the Chambers of Medicine a little while later. He worried about how to explain what had happened. If he told his mom everything then she might think he was too foolish to go see the Sword of Fire. After all, they were never allowed to go cliff jumping without supervision.

Eventually Geneva came out and sat down next to Jack. Then she asked, "What happened?"

"Uh…well…I think…umm…I think that Red Thorn Ranger tried to kidnap us," said Jack.

Geneva abruptly stood up and stormed off. She had to tell George what had happened to their children! She knew George would find the villain and bring him to justice one way…or another.

Chapter 2
Mack's Tale Begins

Mack, a firstborn Cainite, felt miserable. He wanted to run away. But he simply sat and stared at the dying embers of last night's campfire and watched the sun peek over the mountains. He was a wiry kid for his age and wore a ragged red shirt with black pants. He also wore a tattered tan backpack carrying his treasured boomerang.

Mack's left forearm hurt because the Mark of Cain had just been scarred into his arm. His father, Marco, had made the big "X" to celebrate Mack's twelfth birthday. Mack rarely saw his father. Marco was normally out hunting in the miserable mountains of the Lands of Noor.

Suddenly Mack heard a scary sound and turned

just in time to be drenched by a big bucket of water. His older sister, Melissa, laughed as she dropped the bucket. She liked to frighten Mack with stories about velociraptors. They started arguing until their mother, Mara, hollered at them to be quiet.

Mack was about to look for breakfast when his father told him to get into a camel-drawn wagon. It was time to visit Draco, Mack's grandfather, who lived in the city of Narl. Narl was Draco's capital. The tyrant ruled his Lands of Noor with an unjust hand.

Mack was worried as he got into the wagon. Draco had invented the branding ceremony and its quest during some Civil War for some reason. It didn't make sense to Mack. But now it was Mack's turn to go somewhere and prove something to someone. Mack pulled out his boomerang from his backpack. He figured he would need it soon.

Marco whipped the camel to get it moving. It let out a yelp that startled Mack's sister. She banged her head on the lid of an empty barrel.

"Scared of a camel?!" said Mack.

"I hope raptors eat you for breakfast!" said Melissa as she chucked a rock at him.

Mack threw his boomerang and knocked the

rock right out of the air. Then he stood up, caught his boomerang, and raised his fists in triumph.

"Sit down!" said Marco as he and Mack began their long ride down out of the mountains.

* * *

Marco stopped the wagon without warning a couple of hours later. He handed the reins to Mack, then jumped off the cart, grabbed his spear, and slowly walked down the trail. Suddenly a large cougar burst from behind some rocks and charged straight toward Marco. He aimed and speared it at the last second.

Marco cooked and ate the beast without sharing any of it with Mack. Then he climbed back into the wagon, opened a jug of something strong and wrong, and chugged half of it down. Soon he was laughing at everything, but nothing was funny.

* * *

Marco and Mack eventually arrived at the grim and gray city of Narl. It was built right over the Tigris River. The cruel and careless Cainites used its rapids as a sewer system.

They finally stopped at the dreary and dreaded stone palace of Draco. Marco watched Mack jump out of the cart. Marco tried to do the same. He managed to step off, get tangled in the reins, and crash to the ground. His son laughed at him. So Marco chucked an empty bottle at his son. But Mack just ducked and took off.

* * *

Mack wandered around the squalid city streets looking for food. He finally stole a bowl of raw frog legs but got sick from eating them. Then he watched a squad of rough and tough Red Thorn Rangers march past him toward a tall and terrible idol. All the soldiers were bald and wore black and red, representing darkness and fire. Their black shields were painted with red thorns and they carried long black spears with red tips.

Mack fingered his boomerang. He had painted it black with thin red stripes, just like the colors of his heroes. He wanted to be a Red Thorn Ranger someday. They could do anything they wanted!

"Let's go see Draco!" said Marco, as he walked up rubbing his forehead. Then he noticed Mack's fascination with the Red Thorn Rangers. That brought back some bitter memories. "Don't get your hopes up, kid. Dreams come here to die."

* * *

Mack looked at an unfinished painting of pterodactyls on the top floor of Draco's palace later that day. Some really bad artist had given them red and black feathers. The pterodactyls formed a long border around three paintings. He looked at the first painting. It had a soggy swamp with some slimy creature crawling out of it. A second painting showed the creature turning into a monkey. A third painting had the monkey turning into a man. Mack tried not to laugh at the idea of a monkey becoming a man, but it was such a silly idea!

As Mack wondered about the paintings, he could hear his father arguing with some doorkeeper outside the double gold doors of Draco's throne room. His dad had taken Mack right up to the front of a very long line of people. But Marco knew he could get away with it because he was the first-born son of Draco.

Kaligu, the portly doorkeeper, hated Marco's cocky attitude. He also knew Marco would not dare go into the throne room unannounced. Marco had fallen out of favor with Draco after failing at his own quest decades ago. After stalling as long as he dared, Kaligu finally left to tell Draco that Marco and Mack had arrived. Eventually the doorkeeper returned with a welcome and a warning. Draco would see them, but would not allow Mack to speak in the throne room. Kids had to be quiet!

* * *

Mack and Marco walked through two sets of gold-plated doors into the throne room. Red and black curtains hung everywhere, blocking out all natural light. Torches flickered in the darkness. The marble floors and pillars had a peculiar black hue, with red thorns etched in them. Strange people walked and whispered in the dark.

Draco sat on a gold throne at the far end of the room. The bald, black-bearded tyrant had a deep, dark scar shaped like a huge X across his entire face. He wore a black robe embroidered with red thorns and a new crown made of gold.

As Mack and Marco walked toward Draco, a woman named Delilah left. Marco quietly complained that she was Draco's second wife. Marco's mother had died years ago and Marco suspected Delilah had something to do with it. They reached Draco and bowed low to the ground.

"Who is this kid?!" asked Draco.

"Your grandson," said Marco.

"Prove it!" said Draco.

Mack pulled up his sleeve revealing the Mark of Cain on his arm.

Draco looked at it and asked Mack, "Do you like the Mark of Cain? It is quite an honor!"

Mack froze. Then he just nodded.

"What is his quest?" asked Marco. He suddenly realized that Kaligu had lied to him about kids having to be quiet in the throne room.

"Mack," Draco said to the boy, "my twin brother, Daniel, owns a magical white staff. Bring it to me! Then I might let you become a Red Thorn Ranger. Just don't fail me like your father did!" Draco sneered at Marco and dismissed them both with a wave of his hand. Then Draco decided to finish his pathetic painting of peculiarly feathered pterodactyls.

* * *

Mack stopped just outside of the throne room and said, "Draco's scary."

"Stop talking! Someone could hear you," said

Marco. Then he saw Kaligu walking away. "You've got your quest," Marco said to Mack. "Let me know how it turns out." Marco clenched his fist and followed Kaligu around the corner.

Mack stood in a stunned silence. His father had just left him to do it all on his own?! What a guy. What a day.

* * *

Rog and his Nethog cavalry corps left the Neth volcano far behind. They traveled north across the desert. Their crazed carnotaurs raced faster than ever before. A normal man could never make the journey in one night or even ten. But they were more than mere men. They were supernaturally sinister giants bent on revenge! Sand soared high into the air as they galloped on and on toward war and the end of the world.

Chapter 3
Jack's Apology

George rode up ahead of the search party, looking for Eli. Then he saw something. He jumped off his dinosaur and ran up a hill to Eli's half-buried body. Eli's campsite was demolished.

"What happened?!" asked George, brushing dirt from Eli's bushy white beard.

"…Behemoth…" said Eli.

Daniel and his Blue Buccaneers arrived moments later. They hopped off their dinosaurs and joined in the digging. Daniel glanced up at a long trail of demolished trees that went straight through the campsite. The world's largest dinosaur must have surprised Eli with a sudden stampede.

Suddenly a messenger rode up to the rescue

party and said, "George, a Red Thorn Ranger tried to kidnap your kids!" George raced for home without a word.

* * *

Jack missed the target every time as he practiced with his slingshot after lunch. With his brother hurt, and his great-grandpa missing, it didn't occur to him that lying to his mother might be part of the problem with his aim.

George rushed into the courtyard and asked, "Jack, are you ok?!"

"I…uhh…well-" began Jack, but then trumpets announced Eli's arrival at the front gate. They both saw Grandpa Daniel rush Great-grandpa Eli to the Chambers of Medicine.

"What's going on, Dad?!" asked Jack.

"Eli was sort of stepped on by the world's biggest dinosaur," said George.

"What about my pilgrimage?!" asked Jack. He turned to his dad, but George had already gone.

* * *

Jack wasn't allowed in the Chambers of

Medicine, so he wandered up to the top of his dad's prayer tower. But Jack didn't know what to say to God. So he simply leaned on the railing and watched an eagle fly in the sky.

"It's tough sometimes," said Sarah as she came up the steps.

"What's tough?" asked Jack.

"Waiting is tough…"

Jack listened to Sarah for a few seconds, then tuned her out. He didn't need a nanny! Jack saw pterodactyls swoop in and swarm the solitary eagle.

"…make sense?" asked Sarah.

"What? Oh…yeah, I guess," said Jack.

"Good. Don't worry. I'm sure something will work out," smiled Sarah as she headed down the stairs. She had spent a lifetime waiting to get married until Ben, the Captain of the Guard, had come along and proposed to her.

Jack watched the pterodactyls attacking the eagle and took out his slingshot. He couldn't get a clear shot without hitting the bird! When the right moment came he fired and hit a pterodactyl. It went down and the rest scattered. Soon the eagle was soaring again. Jack wished he were an eagle. They had it easy!

* * *

Karl, the Red Thorn Ranger, was a man on a mysterious mission and now on the run! He wanted to get as far away as possible after his accidental run-in with those two Sethite boys. He had made it to the abandoned entrance to the Bridge of Peace, but now a herd of triceratops blocked his way.

One of the triceratops stopped, looked up, twitched, and then went back to eating. Karl was careful not to startle it. They could be deadly if surprised. But he was in a hurry, so he reached for his spear…and felt a sharp tickle on his ear!

"Choose your move carefully," warned George holding the spear. Nobody messed with his family and got away with it for long!

* * *

Jack was still worried about Josh and Great-grandpa Eli at dinner time. He barely picked at his food. Then he saw his dad walk into the dining hall, looking very serious.

"I found the Cainite who tried to kidnap you," said George as he grabbed a peach to eat. He motioned for Jack to follow him outside. "The ranger claims he wasn't kidnapping you," said

George. He took a bite of his peach as they both sat down on a bench.

Josh squirmed a bit in his seat and said, "He would have…uh…but…so…oh…I don't know. Josh just slipped."

"Slipped?" asked George, taking another bite of his peach.

"Ok, ok! We went cliff jumping. Josh fell in and maybe that ranger guy was as surprised as we were. Can I see Josh now?" asked Jack, hoping to change the subject.

"Jack, tell the whole truth the first time, especially to your mother. Lying is always wrong. No slingshot for two days or clean the stables. Pick your punishment."

The slingshot was Jack's favorite possession but he really didn't like the mountains of dino doo-doo in the stables. "The slingshot," Jack's shoulders slumped as he surrendered it to his father. "Can we see Josh now?"

"Yes," said George. The two of them headed over to the Chambers of Medicine. But then George was stopped by Daniel to talk about something and Jack went in by himself.

* * *

Jack apologized to his mother in the hall. She forgave him and brought Jack into the room to see Josh. Jack got a little freaked out seeing Josh lying there all bandaged up.

"Sorry about everything," said Jack, sitting on the bed next to Josh.

"…It's ok," said Josh. They tried to joke around. But their mother quickly ushered Jack out the door to give Josh a little peace and quiet.

* * *

Jack decided to practice his slingshot. Then he remembered he was grounded. "I'm bored!" Jack said to no one in particular as he kicked a stone outside the Chambers of Medicine.

"Then let's catch up on your homework," suggested his mom, walking up behind him.

Jack moaned and groaned as they walked over to the Chambers of Learning. He hoped to avoid taking his geography quiz because every place everywhere seemed to start with an "N."

"How about history?" Geneva suggested.

Jack liked history even less than geography. But he had to do something, so Jack pulled out a scroll. Then he read the following paragraph:

> *"The Civil War fought between the Sethites and Cainites ended in 289 A.C. (After Creation). To celebrate the ceasefire, Eli built the Bridge of Peace to cross the Nayer Valley. This bridge connects Daniel's Sethite Lands of Neer with Draco's Cainite Lands of Noor. Mist rising from this valley covers the bridge. This serves to remind us to forgive and forget the sins of the past."*

Josh found it odd that he had to learn about what his relatives had to forget. But he was more curious about something else, so Josh asked, "Why doesn't everyone go see the Sword of Fire?"

"Uh…let's finish this history first," said his mother.

"Ok…why doesn't anyone use the bridge?"

"I guess no one really wanted to start over," said Geneva as George joined them.

"Dad, why doesn't everyone go to see the Sword of Fire? Mom won't tell me."

George glanced at Geneva and said, "Great-grandpa Eli told me that something horrible happened near the Sword of Fire. Most people don't know how to get there now. The few that still do… don't go. They are afraid, and they should be. By the way, Eli wants to talk to you."

"Yes!" said Jack. He jumped off his stool and ran from the room.

"I didn't want to scare him," said Geneva.

"He's going on a pilgrimage…not a vacation," said George. He gave Geneva a gentle hug and left to catch up to Jack.

Geneva put away the scroll. Then her unborn baby started kicking again as she headed back to sit with Josh.

* * *

Jack and George were warned by a doctor not to talk too long with Great-grandpa Eli. The mighty man of great renown was in rough shape.

"How do you feel?" asked Jack.

"I've been better," Eli said. "Jack, I can't take you to see the Sword of Fire."

"What?" said Jack. "Why not?!"

"The steps are too steep," said Eli.

"Jack, Eli asked me take you instead," said George.

"Yes!" said Jack jumping up. "Let's go!"

"That's settles it. Tomorrow we will all head back to the House of Esther," said Eli. He could barely move, but he still wanted to send Jack off on his pilgrimage with the proper ceremony.

* * *

Rog and his Nethog cavalry corps approached a semi-arid sloping wasteland after a long, hot ride across the desert. Rog's two sons, Grog and Magrog, complained as they rode their carnotaurs. They were tired from the desert trek and wanted a break.

Rog's big and bulky sons weren't the brightest, but they were family. That made them a little bit more loyal than the rest of the Nethog. In fact, that was the only reason they commanded the two legions of Rog's cavalry corps. But Rog could care less about his son's actual opinions. So the horde rode on and on as the sons of Rog seethed in silent rage.

Chapter 4
Mack's Elephant

Mack stole a horse. Stealing made him feel sick to his stomach. He somehow knew it was wrong, but at the moment he could care less. Instead, Mack was thinking of being a Red Thorn Ranger one day. They did whatever it took to get the job done! Mack assumed Daniel lived somewhere west, because no one lived near the Lands of Noor in any other direction. So he headed west on a road called Adam's Way.

After traveling for hours and hours, Mack's horse suddenly reared up, tossed Mack to the ground, and ran into the jungle. A huge and hungry allosaurus charged past Mack, hunting the horse for lunch. Mack leapt down the embankment of the

Tigris River to hide but crashed face-first in front of a hungry hippopotamus. Just then the allosaurus came back looking for dessert. Mack rolled clear as the dinosaur chomped down on the hippo. But then the hippo bit the allosaurus just as fiercely!

As the beasts fought each other Mack ran back up to the road, where he was nearly run over by two panicked horses. They pulled a partially wrecked wagon and were being chased by a second allosaurus. Mack grabbed a rope trailing behind the wagon as it raced past him. He scrambled aboard the wagon and right up to its terrified slave driver. The guy tried to shove Mack off, but Mack jumped out of the guy's reach and fell onto a horse.

Suddenly a shadow passed over Mack. A massive pteranodon swooped down and snatched him! It carried him high up in the air as it veered over the jungle toward the river. Mack jabbed his boomerang into the pteranodon's claws. It shrieked and dropped him.

Mack fell into the jungle below. He found himself upside down and tangled in vines high above the ground. As he slowly twisted in a circle a saber-toothed tiger jumped at him from a nearby limb! Mack jerked back at the last second. The tiger's teeth shredded the front of Mack's shirt as the huge cat crashed to the ground.

Then something slimy distracted Mack from above. He looked up to see a massive snake slithering down the vine. Mack whacked at the snake with his boomerang but it still wrapped itself around him. Then Mack heard a roar! The saber-toothed tiger jumped up and clawed the serpent. All three of them struggled in midair for a few seconds until the vines snapped and they crashed to the ground. Mack escaped as the tiger and snake fought each other on the forest floor.

Mack struggled through the dense jungle back to the road and freaked out! Apparently the pteranodon had flown him right back to where the two allosaurs had first hunted the horses. Then Mack saw the two allosaurs again.

This time one allosaur was dead and covered with ropes and spears. Cainite hunters were busy trying to pull the second one down too. It roared and swung its head from side to side. Hunters were hurled every which way as they hung on to their ropes. Then Mack noticed a lazy Cainite soldier watching the action from further up the road while sitting on an elephant. That gave Mack an idea! He sprinted past the hunters and up to the soldier. Mack showed him the "X" on his arm and demanded the elephant for himself. The grumpy soldier took one look at the Mark of Cain and quickly obeyed.

Suddenly, Mack felt a little too cocky for his own good. Then Mack heard a loud thud. The second allosaur had just gone down. While the soldier was distracted by the gruesome spectacle Mack took off down the road, riding the elephant.

A few minutes later his adrenalin wore off and he puked from all the stress. He suddenly wondered why he should risk his life to get some dumb stick. It was too dangerous and nobody at home wanted him around anyway. Mack decided to quit the quest and just run away!

* * *

Mack got hungry after riding west for a couple more hours, so he decided to go spear fishing. He climbed down from his elephant and carved a spear from a tree limb. Soon he stood on a massive boulder leaning out over the raging Tigris River. He tied a long vine to his new spear and wrapped the other end of the vine around his waist. Then Mack spotted turtles sunning themselves on a log leaning out over the rapids.

Mack climbed down the boulder and out onto the log to spear one. But he slipped and fell into the raging river. The fierce current swept him along until he felt a ferocious tug. His spear, still tied by the vine to his waist, had jammed in the rocks of the riverbed. The raging current pulled him under and started drowning him.

Mack tugged on the vine again and again until he just about ran out of air. Finally, the vine snapped, and he shot to the surface. This time the rapids hurled him toward a big rock in the middle of the river. He felt something nibble at his leg. He scrambled up on the rock and saw piranha swimming all around him!

Mack looked to the sky, half-hoping for another pteranodon to fly by and pick him up. But that didn't seem too likely with the thick tree cover. The trees did give him an idea though. He pulled what was left of his vine out of the water. After tying it to his boomerang he chucked it up and over an overhanging branch. He pulled hard on the vine to check the branch's strength. The branch snapped and dropped straight down toward him! He jumped out of its way only to fall back into the piranha-infested water.

Mack scrambled out of the water and back on

the rock. He wondered why the piranha had ignored him when he saw the reason. A brontosaurus was casually crossing the raging rapids. The piranhas were now swarming it instead of him!

Mack whipped his boomerang up and over another branch. He yanked it hard, and this time it didn't break. He climbed up the vine to the branch and looked back. The brontosaurus was slowly stomping the last of the vicious little fish deep into the river bottom.

The dinosaur looked around, leaned over, and slowly began to chew the leaves on Mack's branch! The branch slowly swayed Mack up and down. He held on tight, desperate with fright. When the branch started to crack he inched along until he dropped into some deep mud and slogged to shore. The elephant was nowhere to be found, so he headed west, walking on the road.

* * *

Mack felt like he had been walking forever when he heard noises like a party around the next bend in the road. It was getting dark and he was starving, so he quietly crept up to the large tent pitched by the road. On the way to its entrance he stole a cloak from some baggage to blend in with the crowd. He was about to peek inside when a girl about his age walked out with her big sister. She wore a pink vest. Mack didn't know what to say. But she did.

"You stink."

"Hush up, Natalie! You're such a child," said the older girl. Then she took one look at Mack and dragged him inside.

She took him to a young guy with slicked back black hair. He sat in a chair strumming a stringed instrument. His bare feet were propped up on a table. He looked at Mack and said, "Hi, my name is Simon…you're a mess, kid!"

"I haven't eaten in days," Mack said.

"Then chow down! No rules here, man. It's all free!" Simon stood up and wandered off trying to look cool while doing so.

Mack ate and ate until he noticed Natalie sitting there staring at him eat like a pig.

"Where are you going?" asked Mack.

Natalie began twirling her red hair. "Mom thinks we're on our way to see Jack's send-off ceremony. But Nicole, that's my big sister, says a pilgrimage is just a bunch of macho male nonsense. So, we're heading to the city of Narl with Simon.

That's Nicole's boyfriend. But I don't think Simon knows that he is her boyfriend just yet. Did you know Simon says that the city of Narl has no rules and lots of free food?"

Mack burst out laughing. Bits of food went all over the place. He had no idea who Jack was but he did know there was no free food in Narl. He was about to tell her that when a dozen velociraptors burst into the tent from everywhere!

Mack froze. He saw Natalie screaming at him. Finally she dragged him outside in the chaos, where Nicole scooped them both up on the back of a galloping horse. She took off back for home with two raptors in hot and hungry pursuit.

Mack desperately leaned from side to side as raptors snapped at him again and again. One snagged his stolen cloak and started to pull him off the back of the horse. Mack yanked the knot loose. The cloak flew off and flopped over the raptor's head. It stopped to free itself.

The other raptor bit at Mack's boot. He kicked that raptor in the nose with his heel, but it didn't stop. Mack yanked out his boomerang and whipped it over Natalie and Nicole's head.

The boomerang came whizzing back. All three of them ducked and it whacked the last raptor right between the eyes. The raptor went down as Mack leaned backwards and caught his boomerang. The dazed raptor stood up, shook itself, and looped back toward the tents in search of easier prey. Mack, Natalie, and Nicole were safe…for now.

* * *

Grog and **Magrog** were sure their soldiers would be allowed to take a much-needed break after crossing the wasteland. But their father ordered them to go faster! The mountain range dividing the Known Lands into the Lands of Neer and Noor was up ahead. He wanted to be in its Nayer Valley as soon as possible.

Grog and Magrog gave each other a grumpy look. After pouting and pondering their problem they both began thinking thoughts only supernaturally sinister giants would think.

Chapter 5
Jack's Fall

Jack hid under a table, listening to his dad talking with Ben and Grandpa Daniel after breakfast the next morning. The caravan was ready to go but the three Sethites were still debating about what to do with Karl the Cainite.

Finally George told Ben to take Karl to the Bridge of Peace and just release him. Ben frowned and was about to object when Geneva entered the room. Ben and Daniel left the hall to give George and Geneva a moment of privacy. But Jack stayed hidden under the table, listening to his parents.

Geneva told George that she wanted to stay home because her due date was so close and Josh was in no shape to travel far anyway. George had an embarrassing secret that made going on the quest difficult for him as well. So, they prayed together for traveling mercy.

Jack slipped out unseen and waited at the front of the crowded caravan in the courtyard until his dad showed up. They mounted their dinosaurs and followed just behind a parade of Blue Buccaneers carrying huge blue and white Sethite banners. Jack's mother smiled, waved goodbye...and prayed again!

* * *

Jack daydreamed later that day. He knew one day he would join the Council of Heirs because he was a firstborn son. So he felt like a king of all the Known Lands as he rode his dinosaur. But then Jack happened to think of his obnoxious cousins traveling with him. Bill, Butch, and Bob were triplets and a bunch of bullies.

"Jack…Jack?...Jack!" said George.

Jack stopped daydreaming. "What?"

"What are you thinking about?" asked his father as he rode up to Jack. But Jack was too embarrassed to actually say anything. So George eventually said, "Never forget we are not that much different from the beggars back home."

"...Ok," said Jack, unsure of what his father meant. A beggar's son didn't get to go see the Sword of Fire. Jack watched his father ride ahead. Then someone else called out his name.

"Jack? Oh...Jack? Can you hear me?" said Bill, as Butch and Bob laughed.

"What do you want?!" asked Jack as the bullies rode up and surrounded Jack.

"Are you bored?" asked Bill.

"No..." said Jack.

"Riding all day long isn't boring to you?" asked Bob.

"Jack's not bored because he thinks he is going to boss us around someday," said Bill.

"Are you bossy?!" asked Butch, shaking his fist at Jack.

Jack ignored them all and kept on riding.

"Jack's not talking to us," said Bill.

"Are you too good for us?!" asked Bob.

Bill noticed Daniel riding up behind them so he turned to Jack and said, "Talk to you later, pilgrim. C'mon guys, this is boring!"

"Well done," said Daniel, watching the triplets drift back into the caravan.

"I wanted to punch them all," said Jack.

Daniel laughed and adjusted his staff in its

harness. "I know what you mean. I punched once when I should have turned the other cheek."

"The Civil War?" asked Jack.

"Yes. I wasn't about to let Draco do to me what Cain had done to..." Daniel's voice trailed off. Then he changed the subject. "We are staying overnight in Havilah. Your great-grandpa needs a break from these rough frontier roads."

Jack was disappointed. He had hoped they would go straight to the city of Noss. Grandpa Daniel's capital city was really fun. But Havilah was just a maze of deep gold mines dug all over the place. Staying there usually meant a miserably long visit with his Uncle Matt. He was the richest goldmine owner in the region, with an ego to match. His spoiled rotten daughter, Kelli, was even worse. Jack and Kelli never got along...ever!

* * *

Jack got his slingshot back from his dad at breakfast the next morning. Since he had a couple of hours before the caravan was supposed to leave, he found a place to practice. As he shot a few rounds downrange his cousin Kelli ambled up. She slyly took a round gold nugget out of her pocket and gave it to Jack. Somehow it seemed heavier than gold.

Jack looked for a target and saw chattering monkeys in the treetops along the ridge nearby. He paused. Kelli wondered aloud why Jack didn't shoot at them. Jack explained he was only supposed to shoot at animals when they threatened people. Kelli pointed to coconut trees beyond the monkeys. Jack agreed and sent the nugget soaring from his slingshot. The nugget went farther and faster than he had ever seen.

Jack eagerly asked for more nuggets and Kelli casually agreed to show him where to get more. A few minutes later they peered down the dark shaft of a long abandoned gold mine. A broken basket once used to carry people up and down the shaft swung precariously over the pit.

Suddenly the triplets stepped from their hiding place and dared Jack to get in the basket. Bill offered to use the basket's frayed rope and pulley system to lower him down to get the gold. When Jack refused to do it, they called him a coward. Of course Jack was afraid to go down there. There might be bats, he couldn't see the bottom, and the basket looked broken anyway.

Bob suggested that even Kelli was brave enough

to get into the basket. Kelli was supposed to be in on their joke, but she wasn't listening. She stood staring at a huge black bear lumbering out of the nearby caves! It was irritated by swarming bees. When the beast roared, everyone but Jack took off running in different directions.

Jack saw Kelli trip over a rock. She shrieked in pain. The angry bear charged toward her. She clutched her ankle, screaming at the top of her lungs. Jack instinctively whipped out his slingshot and sent a stone sailing into the bear's side. The bear stopped. Another shot to the bear's shoulder really ticked it off. It turned and ran straight at Jack. Jack fumbled for more ammo as the bear reared up on its hind legs and roared. That gave Jack the second he needed. He fired a stone right between the bear's eyes. The stunned beast fell forward and crashed onto Jack. Then they both tumbled down the mineshaft.

* * *

Jack woke up in total darkness on a wobbly wooden platform built into the side of the mineshaft. He wondered how far he had fallen. He felt around but could not find any way to climb up. Thankfully the bear was gone. As he shifted his position, Jack heard the clatter of stones slip off the platform. He listened for them to hit bottom, but heard nothing. One wrong move and he would fall to his death!

Jack honestly didn't know where he would go if he died. Would he go to Heaven? He had just saved his cousin from a bear. But he also lied and had a lousy attitude at times. He knew the right answers about God's justice, mercy, and grace. But he just didn't know if he really believed it all.

Jack looked up in despair and saw a torch tumbling down toward him. The light fell closer and closer. He reached out to grab it, but missed. Then he heard his father calling for him from above. Suddenly Jack heard another sound, but it didn't come from above…it came from below. A second later Jack was surrounded by hundreds of bats. The torch had startled them from their haunts! He pressed against the shaft wall and swung his slingshot around to keep the bats away. His dad hollered that he was almost there as Jack's frantic movements caused the platform to creak and crack.

Jack's dad told him to jump. Jack hesitated. He couldn't see his father in the darkness. Again George told him to jump. Just as the platform completely collapsed, Jack took a leap of faith.

For a moment Jack was in a frantic free-fall! Then George caught him and hauled him into the basket. He apologized for dropping the torch but Jack was just happy to be alive.

* * *

Uncle Matt hosted a large and lavish banquet later that night to honor his nephew for saving his daughter's life. Jack sat in the place of honor. Matt quieted the crowd and motioned for his daughter to speak. Kelli stood up, leaning on her crutches.

"Jack saved my life today," Kelli began.

The room erupted in applause and a standing ovation. Jack's uncle handed his nephew a big bag of round gold nuggets. A little while later the party began to wrap up as people left.

"This party was so boring," said Bill as the triplets walked past Jack and Kelli.

"You're boring!" Butch said to Bill.

"Jack is a hero!" said Bob wrestling Bill into a headlock.

"Wow," said Kelli as the triplets left.

"Yeah," Jack agreed.

* * *

Rog jumped off his tired carnotaur and ordered his exhausted sons to halt the cavalry corps. Grog and Magrog gave the signal and two thousand weary warriors and their carnotaurs came to a stop.

The Nethog dismounted and stretched. They were deep in the mountains of the Known Lands. First, they fed their dinosaurs something that did not smell like them. Then they doused their heads with ash and painted their skin green again so they would still look scary.

Rog took his two sons up a rocky incline. The fog-shrouded Bridge of Peace, that crossed the Nayer Valley, could just barely be seen in the gathering darkness to the north. Tiny campfires dotted both ends of the bridge. Rog ordered Grog and Magrog to wipe them out.

Grog and Magrog whispered to each other for a while as they walked. What they were planning would just have to wait until they won this little battle first. It was a battle they had no doubt they would easily win.

Chapter 6
Ben's Courage

Ben, the Captain of the Guard, frowned as his Blue Buccaneers escorted Karl, the captured Red Thorn Ranger, to the Bridge of Peace. It was a long walk made longer because they had to wait until after sunset for a herd of triceratops to finally clear out of their way. After the herd ambled off, the soldiers marched up to the three stone arches that formed the entrance to the nearly abandoned Bridge of Peace. A small Sethite garrison stationed at the bridge's entrance greeted them.

Ben released Karl at the center arch. Karl was less than appreciative and made his opinions vividly known before running off into the dark, swirling fog. Ben ignored Karl's rant and noticed his lieutenant peering over the railing on the bridge. The nervous lieutenant could hear fearsome carnotaurs bellow somewhere in the darkness below them. But the sound of dinosaurs was nothing new to Ben.

* * *

Ben decided to take the Blue Buccaneers down to the decaying Peace Pavilion, midway down the bridge. He wanted to make sure the Red Thorn Ranger was really gone. Two single-file rows of Blue Buccaneers began their march. They moved carefully and quietly along the Sethite flags that lined the sides of the bridge in the dark fog. Ben trudged down the center of the bridge, frowning as he walked. He was a serious soldier. The frontier was no place for fun, but he thought this mission would be about as dangerous as a walk in the park. He had never been more wrong.

* * *

Marco chewed on a big turkey leg, but was too tipsy to notice it was raw. He sat staring at the Cainite entrance to the Bridge of Peace. The two smaller arches were completely bricked up with just the center arch still open. Marco had just arrived after being exiled here by Draco for punching Kaligu in the jaw. But Marco suspected Delilah was really behind his father's decision. He looked around at the few hundred guards posted at the edge of the frontier, either asleep or bored.

Deep down Marco wanted Draco's respect and would have done anything to get it. But it was too late now. Or was it? Marco decided to prove to his father that he was fit to command the Red Thorn Rangers. He would heroically patrol the bridge! He ordered a squad to follow him. But they just ignored him. So Marco wandered alone until he began to feel sick from the turkey. He leaned over the south side of the bridge to throw up. But before he could, he panicked at what he saw coming up at him through the darkness.

Grog and Magrog swarmed up and all over the Red Thorn Rangers. The two supernaturally sinister giants carried huge crossbows and shot everywhere. Magrog watched Marco flee down the bridge. The giant took aim with his massive crossbow and pulled the trigger. Marco took a hit to the shoulder. He tumbled down, but got up and stumbled on. Magrog shot again into the fog just for the fun of it.

* * *

Ben frowned as the whistle of a crossbow bolt sliced through the fog just above his head. The Blue Buccaneers dropped silently to the ground as they heard strange war cries. At Ben's signal the soldiers sprinted forward to the Peace Pavilion to take cover. They hid behind black marble memorial pillars built in a large circle around the Flag of Heirs. Their slings and stones were ready for action.

Marco stumbled toward Ben and the Blue Buccaneers through the fog. Ben frowned yet again when he realized the man wasn't Karl the Cainite. Marco quickly complained that he had been shot by green-skinned giants. The smell of something strong and wrong was so bad that Ben asked Marco if he was drunk. That angered Marco, who impulsively took a swing at Ben. But Ben ducked and decked Marco with a quick blow. Marco fell to the ground, unconscious. Then Ben's lieutenant quickly bound the Cainite and bandaged the scratch on Marco's shoulder.

Ben ordered his lieutenant to run home and warn them that something supernaturally sinister was coming. A moment later Grog blitzed out of the fog and crushed everyone in his path.

Ben, the last survivor, jumped off the bridge from the space between two Sethite flags. Then he turned and made a desperate snap with his whip. It curled tightly around a flagpole, causing him to swing wildly back and forth under the bridge.

Grog ran over and started pulling the whip up hand-over-hand. Then Magrog jogged up, picking his teeth with a tiny turkey leg he had found. He looked over the edge as Grog pulled up the last of the whip. They both laughed at the thought of the little man falling to his death.

Ben fell until he crashed into an archaeopteryx nest. That sent the birds flying! The nest rested on an ornamental stone dove decorating a supporting pillar. He mourned the loss of his men. He had failed to protect them! Ben had to do something soon or more people would suffer. Ben heard the giants celebrating above him. So he decided to climb back up through the fog and listen to their battle plans.

* * *

Rog walked along the bridge, casually snapping Sethite flags like twigs and tossing them over the side. He saw his sons talking in low tones up ahead so he walked over to them.

"Grog and Magrog, take your legions and wipe out the Lands of Neer and Noor. Then get to the rendezvous point. When I have the Sword of Fire… the Nethog shall be avenged!"

Grog and Magrog watched their father rant. They thought he had finally gone crazy. None of the Nethog actually believed the Tales of Eden. Regardless, Grog and Magrog had two thousand giants and their carnotaurs to hoist up on the bridge. That would take time, even for them. They were exhausted, and so were their troops. They decided they would attack when they were good and ready.

* * *

Ben had heard enough. He had to get home and get Sarah to safety. He saw his whip and grabbed it after the giants left. Then he sprinted off the bridge, hoping to catch up with his lieutenant. He made it quite far before blundering right into a triceratops. The triceratops looked at Ben, lowered its head and charged. Ben rolled out of its way and right into his lieutenant. The man had been trampled by the triceratops. No one at home knew an attack was coming!

The triceratops skidded to a stop, turned, and charged at him again. Ben took out his whip and nipped the charging triceratops right on its nose. It stopped, blinked, and charged again. Ben ran right at the beast. The triceratops stopped. Then it let out a roar. Ben did the same. When the dinosaur snorted, Ben did too. The dinosaur paused, shook its head, and started nosing through the grass, looking for food.

Ben slowly backed up, thinking he had to get to Sarah right away. But then he slipped on a pile of dino doo-doo. He tumbled backward down a steep hill and knocked himself out cold.

* * *

Ben woke up just before dawn, face-to-face with the triceratops. It looked like it had been killed for fun by the Nethog and pushed down the hill. Then he heard the terrible sound of sinister trumpets. Ben peered through the tall grass and saw a legion of green-skinned giants beginning to wake up. They started strapping on their bulky orange and black armor while others began lining up their carnotaurs. Ben crawled through the grass and then ran headlong for the fortress. The fortress guards let him in just as carnotaurs could be heard roaring in the distance.

* * *

Grog first led his legion of Nethog to the Village of Noll and burned it down, along with all the farms. Then the giants quickly surrounded the fortress and launched fiery volley after volley from their crossbows. Grog dismounted, yanked out a tree from the ground, and used it to pole vault over the fortress entrance. He started to open its doors from the inside when he felt a whip wrap around his arm. That stung!

Ben frowned but stood his ground, holding his whip. The giant laughed and yanked his arm back. Ben flew forward and crashed face-first into the dirt. Grog gripped the whip wrapped around his arm and started swinging Ben high in the air. Ben had to let go and crashed into a wagon filled with burning hay. He rolled out of it, on fire! A woman threw a blanket on him and snuffed out the flames.

"We won't last until dawn here," Sarah said as they watched Grog yank open the doors.

"If you have a better idea now's the time!"

"Deep Drop," she urged.

"Go!" Ben agreed. He found another whip on the ground by the burning wagon and took off. Ben formed the surviving Blue Buccaneers into a perimeter around the fortress tower. He hoped to distract the giants from chasing down the fleeing families. They took the bait!

After stalling as long as he could, Ben led his surviving Blue Buccaneers inside the burning tower. It collapsed just as they raced down into its cellars. He led the way through the maze of storage tunnels and up into the burning stables. Then the soldiers fled the fortress, using a random route to shake off any pursuit.

* * *

Marco struggled to move on the Bridge of Peace. Then Karl the Cainite came up and cut Marco free. Marco demanded to be taken back to the city of Narl. Karl agreed, but turned away to hide his contempt. Karl had rescued this poor excuse for a firstborn heir just to keep all his options open. But he was not going home. He had a mysterious mission to finish first!

* * *

Ben and the last of his Blue Buccaneers climbed up a steep incline to get to the Deep Drop. Deep Drop was a chasm so deep and wide that the raging

Euphrates River looked like a bubbling brook from this height. They got to George's old, rickety rope bridge just as the last of the women and children made it across. Ben ordered his troops to cross the bridge while he paused to protect the rear. He waved to Sarah, standing on the other side.

Ben was about to cross the rope bridge when he heard a supernaturally sinister laugh. He turned to see Grog climbing up toward him. Ben knew if he crossed now Grog would follow. He had to save Sarah and his men! Just as his last soldier made it across he chopped the ropes holding the bridge. He watched it crash and collapse against the far side of the chasm.

Ben saw Geneva pull his weeping wife down the other side, out of sight. He offered up a prayer, and turned to face the supernaturally sinister giants with a final frown.

Chapter 7
Mack's Apple

Mack held on wearily as he rode non-stop with Natalie and Nicole. They were so tired they hardly talked at all. Eventually they reached a massive crossroads at the border between the Sethite Lands of Noor and the Cainite Lands of Neer. A wide road went up north, toward Eli's Land. A narrow road went down south, to the city of Nitt. Massive redwood trees were everywhere. Mack was amazed at the caravans moving in every direction. It was nothing like the empty streets of Narl.

"I need to tell somebody about Simon," said Nicole as she began to slow down their horse.

Mack noticed soldiers wearing green tunics with an image of a yellow tree woven into them. These woodsmen wore dark brown armor under their tunics and carried long bows with quivers full of arrows.

"Who are those guys?" asked Mack. He knew Draco had spies everywhere.

"You've never seen Green Guardsmen before?! They patrol the border," said Nicole. Natalie turned to see if Mack was serious, but he was gone.

* * *

Mack ran through the crowds of people loading and unloading pack animals. He was really tired of Nicole. One big sister in his life was enough. Mack wandered to the back of a caravan pulled by many moose and looked for something to eat. He saw two junior Green Guardsmen anxiously guarding large wagons holding caged rhinos. They were arguing like cousins often do.

"What's going on?" asked Mack.

"Nothing!" said one of them, clearly unimpressed by Mack's ragged appearance.

"Didn't sound like nothing!" said Mack.

The other one interrupted them and said, "Hi, my name is Roger. My cousin Rick and I were trying to decide who is tougher in a fight…Daniel or Draco. Who would you pick?"

"Draco," said Mack, poking Rick right in the chest. "Red Thorn Rangers rule!"

"Daniel's got the Staff of Power, so he's stronger!" said Rick, pushing back at Mack.

"You're both wrong," said Roger, shoving his way between the two hotheads. "Green Guardsmen are stronger because we worship the woods and rescue rhinos."

"Fine!" said Mack, wondering what woods and rhinos had to do with anything. Then he asked, "Have you got any food?"

"We're heading for the Orchards of Enlightenment," said Roger, pulling his hot-headed cousin back toward their post.

Mack thought about apples and walked up to the front of the caravan as it headed south. An hour later they stopped. People left the caravan and wandered reverently among the apple trees. The trees were in well-ordered rows, but otherwise grew wild. There were ripe apples hanging from the trees and rotting ones on the ground. Mack reached up to pick an apple.

"Stop!" said Rick as he ran up to Mack.

"Why?" asked Mack.

"You can't pick them! That hurts the trees. Eat the ones on the ground," said Rick, picking up an apple.

"They're rotten," said Mack.

"No, they're a gift from Mother Nature," said Rick as he took a bite.

But Mack noticed that Rick ate only the unspoiled part. Mack couldn't help grinning.

"What's so funny?!" asked Rick.

"It's just an apple tree," Mack pointed out.

"No, these are the apple trees from the Orchard of Worldly Wisdom," Rick said. Then he hugged one of the trees.

"Did Mother Nature tell you that too?" asked Mack.

"I guess…no…well, I don't know…"

"You don't know a lot," laughed Mack.

"What's going on here?" interrupted a grumpy Green Guardsman walking toward them.

"He hates Mother Nature!" said Rick.

Mack saw he was outnumbered and took off running toward the back of the caravan.

* * *

Mack thought he had escaped and stopped running to catch his breath a few minutes later. He started thinking about Daniel's magical "Staff of Power" that he was supposed to steal. He still wanted to be a Red Thorn Ranger after all.

Mack asked some lady hugging a tree if Daniel lived in the city of Nitt. She said a well-known warrior with that name lived in the city of Noss and sometimes stayed at the House of Esther. But their conversation was interrupted by Rick screaming that Mack hated trees.

Mack took off running again and reached the rhino cages. Rick shot an arrow near Mack as a warning to stay away. But Mack thought Rick was actually trying to hit him. So Mack threw his boomerang at the lock of a rhino cage. The boomerang broke the lock off. Mack caught the boomerang and yanked the cage open.

The rhino took the hint and charged out. It crashed to the ground, then got up and barreled into another wagon holding its mate. That wagon tipped over and the second rhino burst free. Then the two rhinos rammed and wrecked a few more wagons. Soon rampaging rhinos were running everywhere, wreaking havoc in the caravan and wrecking the orchards!

Mack smirked at the carnage. He wasn't really sure if Draco was tougher than Daniel, but he was sure that Red Thorn Rangers were tougher than Green Guardsmen. Then Mack stole a moose in the chaos and rode it back to the crossroads.

* * *

Mack noticed there were even more caravans at the crossroads now. Red Thorn Rangers mixed uneasily with Blue Buccaneers, but they were mostly kept apart by Green Guardsmen directing traffic. Mack liked the size of the crowds as he rode into the merchant square.

It occurred to Mack that he could just disappear in this crowd and forget all about the quest he had already quit once before. Suddenly his moose, spooked by all the noisy crowds, reared up. Mack fell off backward as the moose charged off through the crowd. Then someone tapped Mack on the shoulder.

"Hi Mack, where did you go?" asked Natalie.

"Natalie! Where did you go?" asked Mack.

"Where did I…wait, what?"

Mack wanted to avoid answering her question so he asked, "Are you going home?"

"Yeah," Natalie replied.

"Natalie, hurry up! You're such a child," said Nicole, riding up in a wagon.

Natalie ignored her big sister and said, "We're going to the House of Esther first. Did you want to come with us?"

Mack had nothing better to do, so he asked, "Is it bigger than this place?"

"Are you serious?!" said Nicole. "Yes!"

"Ok, I'm coming," said Mack, taking a seat next to Natalie up front.

"Sit in the back!" Nicole ordered.

As he obeyed, Mack didn't notice Natalie and Nicole staring and then glaring at each other.

Finally, Natalie leaned in close to Nicole and whispered, "Do you want me to tell Dad about your...boyfriend?!"

"Fine! Have it your way. You're such a child!" said Nicole. She reached into her sack and threw a snack at Mack just to make Natalie happy.

"No thanks!" stammered Mack, throwing the apple back at Nicole. He jumped off the wagon and took off.

"What did you do that for?" said Natalie.

"What did I do?!" asked Nicole, taking a bewildered bite of an obviously ordinary apple.

* * *

Magrog led his legion straight into the heart of the Lands of Noor. At midnight they rode their carnotaurs through the raging rapids of the Tigris

River, until they were right under the center of the city of Narl. Then Magrog gave the signal. A thousand giants blew their horrible horns. Then they burst up and out of the sewer system and destroyed everything in their path.

It didn't take long for Magrog to find and bash down the golden doors to Draco's dreary throne room. The place was deserted. Magrog took a torch and lit the curtains on fire. Then a couple of giants ripped Draco's throne from the floor and threw it over a balcony.

Magrog stood on the balcony and looked at the smoking ruins of the city. He was sort of disappointed. The Red Thorn Rangers had a fearsome reputation, but it had turned out to be a false one. The battle was almost over before it had even begun. Conquering the Known Lands would be even easier than he had thought. He finally decided that he would, in fact, overthrow his crazy father and rule over all the Known Lands…with or without his younger brother.

* * *

Draco and his surviving bodyguards gathered with a dozen or so panicked women and children outside a little-used gate. They could hear the supernaturally sinister giants getting closer and closer. The Nethog were raging and wrecking everything as their carnotaurs roared.

"I and my Red Thorn Rangers will fight the giants so you can escape," said Draco.

"Where are we going?" asked Delilah.

"Kaligu will take you to a hunter's camp in the mountains to hide," Draco said. "You will be safe there until we can join you."

"Safe?" asked Mack's mother. Mara and Melissa had just returned to Narl because they had not felt safe in a hunter's camp without Marco and Mack around.

"Silence!" Draco demanded.

Kaligu also wondered about the plan. It meant riding east, within sight of the outer city wall, where the battle still raged. But no one dared question Draco. The temperamental tyrant was difficult and dangerous if disobeyed. So Kaligu took the women and their children and rode east, just like they were told.

"How is that way safer?" asked a Red Thorn Ranger.

"Who cares? They're bait!" said Draco.

Chapter 8
Jack Sets Sail

Jack was tired of riding. After leaving Havilah the caravan had picked up Grandpa Daniel's wife, Grandma Deborah, and most of their children from the city of Noss. Jack liked that the buildings in Noss had been constructed with a careful concern for nature. Then, at the crossroads near the city of Nitt, they had watched Green Guardsmen try to catch rhinos running all over the place. But now their caravan traveled north, through yet another forest.

Suddenly Abel's Wall came into view. It had huge guard towers and stretched across the entire width of the peninsula of Eli's Land. In fact, Abel's Wall went right out into the middle of the raging headwaters of the Euphrates River to the west and the Tigris River to the east. The wall had been built to keep out the Behemoth.

The caravan passed slowly through the massive wall's only gate because the place was packed with people. Eli's police force, known as Purple Peacekeepers, directed traffic through the gate. They wore purple tunics with a silver sword woven into the fabric on their chests. They carried no weapons because they were masters of unarmed combat.

George pointed to a majestic flag on the wall, called the Flag of Heirs. It had solid vertical stripes of black, red, white, green, and yellow. George explained the meaning of each color. Black represented people's sin before a perfect God. Red was the blood of the atoning sacrifice from God. White illustrated the purity believers received when they trusted in God. Green stood for spiritual growth, with yellow standing for the true gold of eternal life in heaven. Jack heard his dad, but he wasn't really listening. He just wanted to see the Sword of Fire.

George understood his son's growing excitement. So, he decided to make it a race to the House of Esther. They galloped up a long road as it wound past farms and fields to a high summit at the northernmost tip of the peninsula.

Soon George and Jack rode through the four front doors of the House of Esther and into an open-air courtyard filled with hundreds of merchants and Purple Peacekeepers. From there they galloped down winding, tree-lined streets. They even passed a zoo with an empty rhinoceros exhibit and perplexed zookeepers.

Eventually George and Jack rode around two tall towers near a beautiful fountain. One tower, long abandoned, belonged to Draco. Daniel used the other tower when he visited his parents. Then they saw the impressive home of Eli and Esther. This tower was built near the northernmost peak of the peninsula and was higher than most of the rest of the House of Esther. They eased off their dinosaurs and stretched. They had finally made it!

* * *

Jack stood with his dad, Grandpa Daniel, Grandma Deborah, Great-grandpa Eli, and Great-grandma Esther behind a curtain the next day. They were on the stage of a massive, white marble open-air amphitheater everyone called Seth's Cathedral. The shimmering Eden Sea filled the early morning horizon behind them to the north. A comfortable breeze rustled through the five-colored flags posted all around the arena.

Jack wore a special Sethite uniform made only for first-born heirs. It had the symbol of a white dove woven seamlessly into the blue shirt. When a trumpet sounded, Daniel's new butler, named Kustodean, pulled back the curtain. The heirs walked out in a straight line and sat in a semi-circle on the stage.

Jack and his dad whispered together until Esther glared at them. A worship leader led everyone in singing about the glory of God. Then that leader prayed and motioned for the thousands of people to sit down. Eli hobbled over to the podium to give a speech.

After Eli finished, George gestured to the sky. Jack looked up. High above them five hang gliders launched from the summit's rocky peak. They flew in wide circles and rolled out their colors. Each glider towed a different color from the Flag of Heirs. Jack was so amazed he almost forgot to leave as everyone left the stage.

* * *

Jack marveled at all the boats out in the harbor

watching his sendoff. Crowds of people thronged the docks behind him as he and his family walked up to a boat.

A special two-man boat fully loaded with supplies floated at the end of the longest dock. It had a mast with a sail in the middle and two sets of oars. There was no cabin, but a large tan tarp covered their supplies in front of the mast.

Eli said it was time to pray. Close family members gathered in a circle around Jack and George. They offered up prayers of adoration, confession, thanksgiving, and supplication. Sam, who was Eli's eight-year-old son and therefore Jack's Great-uncle, offered up a final prayer.

Eli gave George a secret map with directions to the Sword of Fire. He warned George to stay clear of Zach the Zealot, a deranged, self-proclaimed Guardian of the Gate, who might still live near the Sword of Fire.

* * *

George was not a happy man hours and hours later. The Eden Sea was challenging to navigate, especially for a frontiersman-turned-farmer like George. Nor was he fond of what swam below. Eventually George had a moment to talk. He said,

"I promised your great-grandpa I would talk to you about creation."

"Dad, I've heard this all before," Jack said. "Adam pops out of the dust. He names a few animals and can't find a friend…one rib later and it's 'hello Eve.'"

"You've heard what before?" asked George, trying to avoid a floating forest directly ahead of them.

"Before what?" asked Jack, amazed at the gnarled roots that formed the island's entire shoreline. "Anyway, I already know it all. On the first day God created light. On the second day He created the water on the earth and in the heavens."

George managed to avoid the floating forest. So, he was able to ask, "What about the third day?"

"God created all the plants."

"Check that out!" George interrupted.

"What?" asked Jack, looking for the Sword of Fire on the island. Then he saw it. Not the Sword, but the Falls of Eden in the far distance. It filled the entire horizon ahead of them.

* * *

Jack could barely hear anything as they sailed

close to the roaring Falls of Eden a few hours later. So, he had to shout, "Where are we going?!"

"The Steps of Sorrow!" said George, checking his map. "They can't be found unless you know where to find them. Grab your oars!"

Jack obeyed and they clumsily rowed their boat around massive rocks.

"There's the spot," said George, pointing.

"Where?" said Jack. All he could see was a rocky crag covered with dodo birds that blocked their view of the Falls of Eden.

"Right there," said George, guiding them around the crag into a small, quiet harbor cut into its base. They landed and unloaded their gear in the midst of palm trees growing everywhere.

"Let's go!" said Jack, running up a long and winding marble path. George dropped what he was doing and followed. A few minutes later they both stood looking at a seven-foot-tall, white marble monument covered with green ivy.

"That wasn't here last time," said George. He hacked away at the vines until they could see words chiseled into the monument. George read them out loud:

"The first Adam falls

Bringing sorrow to the womb.
The final Adam calls
Bringing hope from the tomb."

Jack was about to ask his dad what it meant when he saw a saber-toothed tiger leaning over the top of the marker.

George reached up and grabbed the decaying skull. Its huge teeth were still lodged in its rotting upper jaw. "The Cainites claim life slithered out of the sea and that these teeth evolved to eat meat. What do you think?"

Jack took the skull and looked at its big teeth. "God created these teeth to tear up coconuts before the curse, right?"

"That's right! We share the same facts," said George, putting the gross skull back up on the monument. "Correctly interpreting those facts makes all the difference."

"Let's camp here tonight," said Jack.

"Good idea," said George, thankful that there was no sign of Zach the Zealot. As they walked back for their gear, George asked Jack about day four of creation.

"That's where it gets strange to me," Jack said. "God made the plants on day three, but the sun and moon on day four. How can plants live without the sun?"

"Maybe it was a way to show God's power over creation. He doesn't need anything to keep everything alive."

Soon George and Jack relaxed after eating a late dinner next to a roaring fire with a great view of the Sea of Eden.

"Tell me about day five before you go to sleep," suggested George, stoking the fire. There would be no sleep for him tonight. He remembered that lions had once roamed nearby.

"God created all the creatures in the sea and the birds of the air," said Jack, with his head nodding. They could see plesiosaurs swimming and pelicans soaring as the sun set on the horizon. At that moment Jack was cleaned up and comfortable… like the calm before a storm.

* * *

Karl felt it first: a slight shaking in the ground under his feet in the gathering darkness. He motioned for Marco to stay hidden. They were about to cross over a ridge on the southern edge of the city of Nitt. Karl was tired of Marco. The firstborn heir constantly complained about the bandaged little scratch on his shoulder. So, Karl went up the ridge alone to look around.

Marco sat on a rock among redwood trees. He was really tired of Karl. The ranger always pushed and pushed him to go faster. Marco was exhausted and wanted something really strong and wrong to drink. He had no idea where they were and wondered why it was taking so long for Karl to return. The shaking turned into a low rumble as Karl hurried back down the ridge to Marco. Then the low rumble became a roar.

Grog and Magrog's legions converged from the east and west at the crossroads of Adam's Way and began destroying the city of Nitt.

Marco ordered Karl to get them out of there. He'd already seen enough of giants to last a lifetime. Karl agreed. If they went a little faster, they might make it to where they were going. If not, they would die.

Chapter 9
Mack's Bumpy Ride

Mack hitched a ride all the way up north through Eli's Land. It occurred to him that he might as well see if he could at least find Daniel's place. But he soon found himself completely lost in the House of Esther. Finally Mack swiped a package and pretended to be a lost Dinosaur Express delivery boy. A nice old lady pointed out Daniel's seven-story tower right behind him. Mack jogged over to the tower but tripped and dropped the heavy package on his toe. Ouch!

Mack limped the rest of the way to Daniel's tower and was dismayed to find there were no doors or windows on the first two floors. There were just massive bricks and a long set of steps zigzagging up to what appeared to be the main entrance on the third floor. Then he saw wide-open windows on the seventh floor. That gave him an idea. Security in the House of Esther was a joke. Maybe he could simply break in and steal the staff. His quest was back on!

Mack stole a hook and rope from a wagon while its clueless owner ate his lunch at a beautiful fountain. But then Mack pricked his finger on the hook and that hurt. Nursing his sore finger and still aching toe he went back to look at Daniel's tower.

Suddenly Mack had second thoughts about climbing the outside of it. That seemed a little crazy, given its height. Then he noticed an abandoned tower next to Daniel's place. It appeared to completely block Daniel's view of the beautiful Eden Sea. Mack broke in and went up to its eighth floor.

Mack decided to wait all day because he did not want to be seen breaking into Daniel's house. As the sun began to set, he tied a rope to the hook. He had to throw it three times before it finally stuck in an arch above one of the many large, open windows. He tied his end to a wooden beam. Then he tugged hard on the rope. It didn't budge. If he didn't look down he would be fine. He just hoped no one was looking up. He put his boomerang on the rope and held on to it.

As Mack started to step out, he looked down at the gap between the two towers and froze. Time seemed to stop. Then he heard people talking somewhere below. Had someone seen him? Mack took the plunge and zipped across nicely until the bumpy rope slowed him to a stop about five feet from the window. Mack's arms started to cramp. He slowly moved himself along by jerking the boomerang forward. That worked, until the stones holding the hook in place cracked from the strain.

Mack fell! He desperately thrust out his boomerang. It caught on the edge of the window sill and slammed him into the side of the tower. Fortunately, the bricks were rough, and he managed to climb them up to and inside the window. He collapsed on the floor, shaking with fear. Then Mack heard people approaching, so he jumped behind a couch.

Two servants hurried into the room. They stood looking out of the window and argued about what they thought they had seen. After they left, Mack snuck down the hallway. He found an exercise chamber and hid in a closet in the corner. He vowed to stay awake until Daniel showed up. Then he fell asleep.

* * *

Daniel liked to work out in his exercise chamber after his morning devotions. He was good with his staff. He parried back and forth with his trainer. No Sethite could touch him in practice. No Cainite could touch him in combat.

Daniel finally put his staff back in its place on the wall and took a break. But his break was suddenly interrupted by a Purple Peacekeeper. The messenger explained that Geneva had just arrived with a few survivors from an attack on the frontier. In fact, reports of giants attacking were coming in from all across the Lands of Neer!

* * *

Mack, hidden in a closet in the corner, couldn't see what was going on in the room. But after hearing a bunch of people suddenly rush out he thought he might finally have a chance to get the staff! He quietly pushed open the closet door. The room was empty.

Mack walked over to the white, seven-foot-long staff carved from hardened gopher wood. He pulled it from its mount. It did not seem magical. It just had writing carved in it that said "Love the Lord" on one side and "Defend the Family" on the other. It seemed to weigh a ton. He tried spinning the stick for fun but dropped it.

Suddenly a door opened and Daniel's butler walked into the room carrying a broom. Kustodean took one look at Mack and asked, "What are you doing in here?"

Mack froze for a second, picked up the staff and said, "I was trying to spin it." That was the truth; now for the lie. "I'm supposed to bring it to Uncle Daniel."

"Oh?" said Kustodean. He did not recognize the boy. But the House of Esther had hundreds of children running around all the time. This was also Kustodean's first month on the job.

"Should I leave it here?" asked Mack.

Kustodean shrugged and said, "Take it to him." It wasn't like the stick was fragile.

Mack left the room and tried to appear relaxed as he walked out of Daniel's tower. People were now everywhere but no one paid him any attention. His plan was working! But an hour later Mack was lost again. Around every corner were more people and more towers and halls and more rooms and endless bridges over gardens, ponds, and pools. It never seemed to end, and he was getting hungry. Mack also worried that Daniel would miss his stick and sound the alarm.

Finally Mack wandered into a huge, open-air market square full of refugees. Everyone was talking and walking in every direction. The place looked familiar. But, by now, everywhere did. In the chaos he thought he could get away with stealing a blueberry muffin from a baker's basket.

"Gotcha!" said the baker grabbing Mack. Then he called out for a guard to help him.

"What now, Joe?!" asked an irritated Purple Peacekeeper. He had no time to deal with Joe the Baker today. Refugees were pouring in from all across the Known Lands.

"This kid stole a muffin from me!"

The guard ignored the baker, looked at Mack, and said, "Why do you have that staff?"

"I'm bringing it to Daniel," said Mack.

"What about my muffin?!" said Joe.

"I forgot to pay for it because I was watching them," Mack said pointing to the refugees.

"Then pay for it!" said the guard as he walked back to his post to help the refugees.

"Ok," said Mack. Then he took off the moment Joe turned his head.

When Joe realized he had been fooled, he was furious. He decided to pay close attention as two girls walked up to his stall. One reached for a blueberry muffin.

"Pay for it first, please," said Joe.

"Put it back, Natalie," said Nicole. "You're such a child." But Natalie wasn't listening to either of them. She thought she had just seen Mack running through the crowd of refugees.

* * *

Mack thought he was near the main entrance to the House of Esther, but wound up lost in an alley blocked by a fence.

"Mack?"

Mack turned around and saw Natalie.

"Where are you going?" she asked.

"I'm a man on a mission," confided Mack.

Natalie noticed Daniel's staff and asked, "What's your mission?"

"I need to get this stick to the front gate."

"Really? I know the way. Let's go!" Natalie led Mack up and up into the House of Esther and farther and farther from its front doors.

"Why do you have that staff?" she asked as they

stopped near a fountain. But Mack wasn't listening. He was looking around.

"Mack?!"

"Where are we?" asked Mack, ignoring her question. Then he recognized Daniel's tower!

"Why do you really have that stick?"

"Umm, my dad, I mean...no, my uncle, wait, no...he...I have it..." began Mack. He was really tired and suddenly he didn't like the idea of lying to Natalie.

Natalie looked at Mack sadly. Suddenly a dozen Purple Peacekeepers, led by Nicole and Joe the Baker, surrounded them. Natalie backed up as the guards closed in all around Mack. He was trapped! A guard took the staff from Mack while another guard cuffed him. Was his quest over?!

* * *

Rog watched five pairs of mammoth elephants strain to pull a massive catapult into place outside the burning ruins of the city of Nitt. All around him the Nethog were cutting down redwood trees to make more of them.

Magrog and Grog walked up arguing with each other. Magrog had noticed that a new patch covered his brother's right eye and was mocking him. Grog was very embarrassed about his fight with Ben at the Deep Drop.

Rog shouted at Grog and Magrog to test the catapult. So they cocked the catapult's arm back and dumped huge pails of burning coals into the catapult's bucket. Then Grog and Magrog pulled the rope that launched it.

Burning coal soared high into the air. Rog smiled with grim satisfaction as the high-flying coal finally hit the ground and started fires everywhere. Soon Rog would burn the placid plains of Eli's Land with unholy fire. He couldn't wait to burn the whole world.

Chapter 10
Jack's Steps of Sorrow

Jack looked at the Steps of Sorrow going up the cliff. He could not see the top of them. Centuries ago the Council of Heirs had chiseled these rough steps out of solid rock. The steps started out easy, but his dad had said that higher up they were much steeper and closer to the falls.

"What's for breakfast?" asked Jack.

"Nothing until devotions," said his dad.

Jack figured as much. Dad always insisted on devotions before breakfast. Better to get this over with so they could eat and go see the Sword of Fire. So Jack said, "I like day six because God created land animals like dinosaurs and…dogs."

"Dogs?" asked his dad, beginning to frown.

Jack remembered his dad had once said that dogs were too expensive to buy because they had to be bred from wolves. So Jack changed the subject. "Dad, do Cainites actually eat meat?"

"Yes."

"Why don't we?" asked Jack.

"God gave Adam and Eve just fruits and vegetables to eat. No meat on the menu…yet. What else happened on day six?"

"God made Adam and Eve!"

"That's right. Eventually they were given a test in the Garden of Eden. Eve was deceived, but Adam just stood there and let it happen. They sinned. We all would have made the same choice."

* * *

Jack put on his climbing gear after a quick breakfast. As his dad checked Jack's harness he said, "Your sandal's loose."

"Ok, Dad," Jack replied. He would strap it down in a minute. He had to count the gold stones for his sling first. They were still so cool. He wanted to be ready to use them at a moment's notice. He tied his slingshot quite securely to his waist and packed his ammo in a bandolier slung snugly over his shoulder.

George went to the base of the stairs and looked up. Then he tossed Jack a rope and said, "Tie it to your harness just like I showed you."

"I don't need a leash," said Jack.

"It's not a leash. It's a lifeline. If you start to fall, I should be able to stop you," said his dad.

"Should?!" said Jack, forgetting all about his loose sandal strap.

After long hours of climbing, Jack wondered how close they were to the top. The steps were now so steep and close to the Falls of Eden that it felt like they were going straight up a cliff on a wet ladder. Then Jack stepped on his loose sandal strap. He tripped, slipped, and fell.

Higher up the steps, Jack's dad felt a sudden hard tug on his safety harness and lost his balance. They both began to tumble. Then George took a hard hit to his knees by landing on a step. He grabbed the safety rope and pulled it up as hard as he could. Jack suddenly stopped falling and swung wildly in and out of the roaring falls.

"Grab the step!" shouted George over the noise of the falls. Jack's momentum slowed and he was able to scramble back onto a step.

"You ok?" asked George, wincing from the searing pain in both of his knees. He was so scared his hands shook.

Jack just nodded weakly. He clung to the steps, soaked to the bone, just trying to breathe.

* * *

Jack and his dad finally made it up to a narrow crack in the side of the cliff called Miqqedem Pass. After lighting a torch, Jack hurried, but George hobbled, down a long tunnel filled with glittering diamonds. It finally opened into a large cavern with abandoned homes cut into the rock. It appeared that Zach the Zealot was long gone.

"How about we take a break here and you finish up creation week?" asked Jack's dad, wondering if his hands would ever stop shaking.

"Ok," said Jack. But then he got distracted by the huge cave paintings all around him. He could see the Days of Creation, the Tree of Life, the Tree of the Knowledge of Good and Evil, the First Family, and a serpent, but no Sword of Fire.

"Well?" asked George.

Jack said, "Sorry, I was looking for a painting of the Sword of Fire...anyway, at the end of the sixth day God saw what He had made and called it very good. Then the Lord rested on the seventh day."

"Right again!" said George. "There was no death before Adam's sin. God called all of His creation good, and death is definitely not good."

"Can we go now?" asked Jack. He was very hungry and quite thirsty, but he wanted to get to the Sword of Fire!

"Yes," said his father, slowly standing up.

Jack and George followed the trail up and out of the caverns. In front of them was a steep and skillfully terraced ridge covered with all kinds of overgrown fruit trees.

George sat down again to massage his sore knees and said, "We're not far now. When I was here last time, Eli told me that believing is seeing. Faith comes first. What do you think of that?" George looked up, but Jack was gone!

* * *

Jack sprinted up the winding path to the top of the ridge. He ignored his dad's frantic calls to stop. The first thing he noticed at the top was the suffocating heat and swirling steam. Jack walked into the remnants of an ancient amphitheater built by the Nethog. It looked like an earthquake must have destroyed the place and now vines covered everything. He noticed two huge marble pillars in the midst of a smashed altar. As he walked up to them he guessed the Council of Heirs must have removed Og's evil altar and replaced it with the pillars.

Jack walked up to the tall white pillars and saw they were covered with carvings of palm trees and pomegranates. The word "JUSTICE" was carved into the left pillar and "MERCY" into the other. The only way to get to the Garden of Eden was to go right between them, because wide pits of spewing hot lava were everywhere else. The pits extended to the left and right as far as he could see. Then he saw it!

Diamonds covered the ground in an enormous circle just past the pillars. A rocky path emerged on the far side of the circle before disappearing into miles of tangled bushes covered with huge thorns. The thorn bushes sloped down into a tree-covered valley. But Jack wasn't looking at them.

The breathtaking valley seemed as deep and wide as the eye could see. Surrounding the valley was a distant ring of fire formed by the hot lava pits, and past them were tall cliffs rising into massive mountains at the misty edge of sight. But he wasn't looking at them either!

Jack stood staring in wide-eyed amazement at two colossal trees rising from either side of the River of Life in the center of the Garden of Eden. One was lush and green. The other one seemed dead.

"Hey Dad, is the green one the Tree of Life?" shouted Jack as he started to step onto the circle filled with diamonds.

"Not so fast," said George, gripping Jack's shoulder. He pulled Jack back behind the pillars. Then he looked at his son, smiled, and said, "Jack… we made it. We actually made it!"

"Let's get closer!" said Jack.

"Closer? The Cherubim will kill you!"

"But I don't see the Sword!" said Jack.

George was so stunned he let go of Jack. How could his son not see the Sword of Fire? It was right there, turning back and forth. If Jack could not see it that meant he did not have a saving faith in God! Believing was seeing. Faith came first. They just stared at each other. Neither knew what to say next and both were shocked by the other's silence.

Finally Jack mumbled, "Let's get out of here." He turned and headed for home. He couldn't believe he had traveled all this way only to see a big empty space of nothing.

"...Ok," said George, still in shock. But he stumbled and had to stop to rewrap his sore knees.

Jack was hot, hungry, thirsty, and so thoroughly confused that he stopped too. He looked around at the remains of the overgrown amphitheater he had ignored before. Maybe this dumpy old place was the real Garden of Eden!

As he waited impatiently for his dad to finish, Jack fidgeted with a gold stone in his pocket. Suddenly he had an idea. He slipped the stone into his slingshot. Then Jack shot a gold stone right between the pillars while his dad looked for something in their backpack.

"Thirsty?" asked George, looking up to offer Jack a jug of water. That distracted Jack for a split second. When he looked back at the pillars he saw nothing. No stone...and no sword.

* * *

Rog celebrated the fall of the Known Lands in the ashes of the city of Nitt. Grog and Magrog threw tattered flags of Neer and Noor at their father's feet. Rog stomped on both banners and the whole horde cheered. He mounted his carnotaur and unfurled an orange and black flag. The banner, with its symbol of a supernaturally sinister green serpent, flew high into the air.

Rog relished the moment. Surely Emperor Og's son, Chogg, would promote Rog above his arch rivals, Mog and Zog, now. But first Rog had to get through Abel's Wall. It had been built to protect Eli's Land from a charging Behemoth. That meant it was too tall to scale and its gate was unbreakable. But there was a third option: the most treacherous of all.

Chapter 11
Jack and Mack Collide

Jack sailed for home in stubborn silence with his father on the Eden Sea. Soon they approached a floating forest. Gnarled roots, growing from swaying green trees, formed the shoreline and made up the entire island. George asked if Jack wanted to stop, but he didn't feel like it. If there was no sword, then everything he had ever been taught was a lie. Worse yet, his dad pretended to see stuff that clearly wasn't even there. Suddenly he felt a bump.

Then the something bumped Jack and his dad again. George, fearing his worst nightmare, jumped to the set of oars in the stern and told his son to steer for the floating forest. Jack grabbed the rudder and promptly steered them the wrong way. The bumping turned into thumping. The boat began to rock. Jack jerked the rudder the right way and they headed back toward the floating forest.

Jack and his dad almost made it when a leviathan burst from the sea and landed on the back of the boat. The sudden motion tossed Jack high in the air, over the sea monster, and down deep into the water. Jack burst to the surface and swam for the floating forest just ahead of him. He touched roots, scrambled up, and looked back.

Jack saw his father clinging to the mast, trying hard to avoid falling into the leviathan's massive mouth. Suddenly a blast of fire burst forth from the mighty creature. Its flames blasted the boat into pieces all over the sea.

Jack waded back into the water and saw his panicked father drowning! The leviathan searched for George but didn't see him yet. Jack dove back in the water and swam toward his dad. As Jack pulled his unconscious father to the surface the leviathan finally saw them both.

The sea monster lunged through the air and came crashing down toward Jack and George. Its huge splash sent both pilgrims sprawling across the gnarled roots of the shore. Jack managed to drag his father to safety. Fortunately the huge sea creature could not get on land and eventually swam away. Jack thought he might hate swimming forever!

Then Jack heard a cackle. He looked up and saw a small, bright yellow pyroraptor run past him. He heard a chorus of cackles and saw a bunch of the vicious little beasts gather just inside the tree line on the edge of the root-covered shore. He whipped out his slingshot and started shooting. He nailed nine of them before the herd took the hint and scurried back into the forest.

Jack tried desperately to wake up his dad. Finally George mumbled something incoherent about being embarrassed that he did not know how to swim. Then Jack heard the cackle again. He looked up as the scavengers swarmed all around him. He shot furiously, but they kept coming and coming. Soon he was out of ammo!

Suddenly the swarming pyroraptors looked out to sea and scattered back into the forest. Jack turned to see purple flags decorated with silver swords on an approaching ship. A Purple Peacekeeper shouted hello and soon they were all safe aboard.

The ship's captain spoke in low tones to George as the ship's physician tended to George's knees.

Jack asked his dad what was going on and his dad said that the world was at war back home.

* * *

Draco arrived at the entrance to the House of Esther in a bad mood. His fancy new robe was ruined and he had lost his new crown somewhere along the way. Normally, he tried to make visits here as unpleasant as possible. But this time he needed his parents' help. Leaving his exhausted Red Thorn Rangers behind, Draco trudged up the broad marble steps to Eli's Audience Chambers. He ignored the statue of a lion resting with a lamb because he despised it.

Draco intended to interrupt the session of the Council of Heirs. But the sergeant-at-arms did not recognize Draco. That angered Draco and he showed his displeasure with a royal temper tantrum. But that didn't work at all. Purple Peacekeepers just escorted Draco into Esther's Chambers of Reflection instead. Her garden had a stunning view of the Eden Sea.

"I am Eli's favorite son!" said Draco as they left him alone to cool off. But he didn't cool off. He was Draco! Instead he paced around his mother's rose-filled terraces. Urns filled with roses of every color were everywhere. But only gold-rimmed urns had the names of her children engraved into them.

A very long time ago Draco had loved planting roses here with his mother. But now he just kicked a chair in his way and stubbed his toe. He picked up the chair and chucked it into a pot full of roses. The gold-rimmed urn cracked. Draco's toe hurt so he decided to sit down to look at it. He yanked the chair out of the broken pot and slammed it hard on the floor. Then he sat down. The chair collapsed and he fell into a heap on the floor! The sudden fall hurt his back.

Draco's mother, Esther, walked into the room. She couldn't believe the firstborn of her twin sons was actually here. Then Esther noticed the damage everywhere. She said, "What did you do now?!"

Draco was unusually quiet. He just sat on the floor, sifting smashed rose petals between his fingers. Then he whispered, "Ma, they burned my city to the ground."

Just then a sergeant-at-arms walked into the room to finally escort Draco into the Council of Heirs. Draco abruptly stood up, glared at his mother, and stormed out.

Esther looked around and noticed the name on

the broken golden urn. It said Daniel. She picked up a broken piece and thought of her twins as tears filled her eyes. She had lost her temper with Draco yet again. They were more alike than she cared to admit.

* * *

Eli and his Council of Heirs were still in emergency session about the village of Noll. Daniel was about to speak when Draco burst in.

"The Nethog rule the world. Eli's Land stands alone. We must fight to the death!" declared Draco, taking his long-abandoned seat. Chaos erupted in the room!

Daniel suddenly wondered if Draco was somehow helping the giants to get even with him for winning the Civil War. Then Daniel shrugged and said, "Dad, what should we do?"

Everyone looked at Eli. He offered up a silent prayer for wisdom. Finally Eli said, "Draco, you have the most experience with these Nethog. Defend Abel's Wall. Daniel, defend the House of Esther. My Purple Peacekeepers will evacuate the women and children back to the First Lands. May God save us all."

As the Council of Heirs adjourned, Eli noticed Daniel and Draco eyeing each other suspiciously. Children could sure break a parent's heart sometimes.

* * *

Marco and Karl joined the last of the refugees fleeing from across the Lands of Neer and Noor. They all rushed through the massive gate of Abel's Wall. As the gate closed, a Purple Peacekeeper directed Marco and Karl to the top of the gate towers. Once there, Marco saw Draco and his grim-faced Red Thorn Rangers taking their positions for war.

Marco wondered why Draco and his men were here and not in Narl. He turned to ask Karl a question, but the man was gone. Suddenly two thousand carnotaurs and their Nethog riders erupted from the forest on Adam's Way! They thundered toward the front gates of Abel's Wall that protected Eli's Land.

* * *

Rog found the gates closed and Abel's Wall

crawling with puny warriors. Red Thorn Rangers high above him blew their horns to sound an alarm. But the Nethog and their carnotaurs drowned them out with a sinister roar. At Rog's command, dozens of elephant-drawn catapults launched death by fire.

"Get me Grogger!" Rog said.

* * *

Mack sat in a cell. He could see his backpack and Daniel's staff leaning against the wall next to a couple of agitated guards. Suddenly someone came in and took all the guards away. An hour later Natalie slipped into the room, dragging Nicole behind her. Natalie managed to find a key and walked over to Mack's cell. But she could not get it open.

"Better to die free," muttered Nicole as she took the key from Natalie and unlocked Mack's cell. She had just learned about the Nethog's invasion.

"Thanks," said Mack, unsure what Nicole meant. He casually walked over and put on his backpack. Then Mack grabbed Daniel's staff and ran from the room. Once outside, Mack sprinted the wrong way up a long flight of steps. He turned a corner and saw a hang glider ready for take-off.

He was at its launch site at the top of the summit that overlooked the harbor. The place was deserted. But Mack could hear Nicole and Natalie hollering somewhere close behind him. He grabbed a hang glider and ran off the cliff!

* * *

Jack felt bitter as he climbed out of the boat in the harbor at the House of Esther. His pilgrimage was over and he hadn't seen a thing. Jack saw that the harbor and docks were filled with people. Purple Peacekeepers were helping them board boats fleeing back to the First Lands.

Jack spotted Josh and his mom coming toward them with Sarah carrying Holly. Soon his dad had everyone in a great big hug. George began to thank the Lord that they were all safe. But Jack didn't want to pray. He peeked and saw Grandpa Daniel and Grandma Deborah rushing down the dock with many of their children.

Daniel waited until they finished praying and then said, "George, I need you at the front doors. I want the rest of you on a boat now."

Jack was about to ask a question when an empty hang glider crashed into him!

Chapter 12
Mack's Anger

Mack limped up a ladder out of the water and collapsed on the dock. He had bailed from his out-of-control glider at the last moment, but now his ankle really hurt. He saw that his glider must have landed on someone. Everyone around it was trying to lift it. Then Mack watched a bunch of people rush back to the House of Esther carrying some injured kid. He looked around frantically and saw Daniel's staff lying on the dock about fifty feet away. It must have slipped out during his free fall.

* * *

Draco and Marco watched the battle while

standing on Abel's Wall. All Draco thought he had to do was keep the Nethog off the wall long enough and he would be a hero. Sure, there was fire flying everywhere from the Nethog's catapults, but at least they were not trying to scale the wall. He realized why when the wall's massive gates began to open.

Draco and Marco ran down the tower stairs. They found a traitor at work in the gear room, slowly opening the gates. Karl the Cainite laughed maniacally. As Rog's "secret weapon," Karl was keeping all his options open. Then Draco and Marco saw a really big giant named Grogger walk up. He pushed the gate the rest of the way open as the Nethog chanted his name.

It was then that Draco and Marco realized they needed to get out of there. They ran from the gate towers and through the village. There they found two panicked Red Thorn Rangers on their dinosaurs. Both Draco and Marco demanded a ride back to the House of Esther. The battle for Abel's Wall was over. The Known Lands had fallen; sorrow was sure to follow.

* * *

Mack's ankle hurt as he crawled toward the

staff back at the docks. He grabbed it at the same time as some old man.

"Thanks!" said Mack.

The old man looked at Mack, "Thanks?"

"Yeah, now I can take it back to Daniel."

"Is that so?" asked the old man.

"He's been looking for it all day."

"Is that so?" asked the old man again, as he noticed Cain's Mark on Mack's left forearm.

"Yeah, whoever finds it, uh…wins a prize!"

"Hmm…" said the old man as he let go of the stick. But he blocked the way off of the dock.

"Yeah, so, he really wants it back. I better go." Mack tried to stand, but his weak ankle buckled a bit and he dropped the staff.

"Let me help you," said the old man as he picked up the staff and offered a hand to Mack.

"Uhh…I'm fine. Can I have it back?"

"You sure you're ok?" asked the old man.

Mack reached back into his backpack and fingered his boomerang. He had one shot. He chucked the boomerang at the old man's head. The guy ducked. Mack waited smugly. But the old man just turned around and caught it.

"Do not try that again, Cainite," said the man as he handed the boomerang back to Mack.

"Why do you think I am a Cainite?!" asked Mack looking around for a way to escape.

"You have Cain's Mark on your arm. That makes you one of Draco's firstborn heirs…why do you really want the stick?!"

"…I'm...uh, well, you see…" said Mack.

"Are you trying to take this stick to Draco?" asked the old man. When Mack didn't answer, the old man gave him a hard stare.

"Yes…mister…sir," said Mack. "If I don't get the staff to him then…he…he will…" Mack was so scared of what Draco might do that he just stopped talking. He was surprised to see the old man seem deep in thought for a moment.

The old man slowly and reluctantly gave the stick to Mack and said, "Give it to Draco as quick as you can. Then get on a boat and get out of here!"

Mack took the staff, listened to the old man's directions to the front doors, and took off. He wondered why Draco was here. Cainites were supposed to hate the House of Esther most of all.

* * *

Mack made it to the front courtyard of the House of Esther at the same time as Draco.

"Get out of my way!" Draco said to everyone as he jumped off his ride. Then Draco stopped and stared at Mack.

Mack dropped to one knee and said, "Draco, sir, here is Daniel's staff." Mack handed the staff to Draco and asked, "Am I a Red Thorn Ranger now?"

"I don't have time for this nonsense!" said Draco, throwing the stick to the ground and storming off.

Mack was stunned. Then he saw his father arrive and dismount a moment later.

"You found the stick?!" said Marco.

"I…I got the stick… I gave it…I got the stick…I... " said Mack.

"What did he say?" asked Marco.

"…He didn't…he didn't want it."

"Not surprised," shrugged Marco as he wandered away, looking for something strong and wrong to drink.

* * *

Mack stared at Daniel's staff. His quest was over. He had done the impossible. But nobody cared. That made him mad! Mack picked up the stick and slammed it down hard. It didn't even bend. Then, as he tried to throw the staff, someone grabbed the other end of it.

Mack spun around and saw the same old man from the docks again. This time the guy was on a magnificent dinosaur. He wore a blue tunic with a white dove on it that covered his shining armor. The old man asked, "Draco didn't want it?"

"No, he didn't!" Mack said. He let go of the staff and stared at the ground. Then he looked up and said, "I…I stole it…I'm sorry…can you take it to Daniel for me?"

"Yes, I can," smiled the old man. Then he turned to the Purple Peacekeepers guarding the four front doors and said, "Open a door!"

"Dad, don't go!" said Natalie as she and Nicole ran toward their father. The three of them hugged and whispered together. Then he rode out.

Mack stood watching the two girls cry. Then he asked, "What's your dad's name?"

"Daniel," replied Natalie through her tears.

"Oh," said Mack. He liked that old man.

* * *

Eli sat in his wheelchair at the top of the entrance to the House of Esther and watched his son, Daniel, ride out alone. Eli, a mighty man of great renown, felt helpless for the first time in his life. His thoughts drifted back to his distant past.

Long before the Civil War, Og and his Nethog had become supernaturally sinister by committing a great sin near the Sword of Fire. But Eli had destroyed the Nethog's evil altar and had defeated Og in single combat. Then the Council of Heirs had banished all the Nethog to the Unknown Lands.

Why had Behemoth stomped on him just when everyone needed him the most? Eli could barely even move. Now the only thing he could do was sit there and pray. So he did!

* * *

Daniel had a moment to actually think about the insanity of what he was doing as he rode toward the Nethog. He knew that there were not enough boats left to evacuate everyone still in the House of Esther. He also knew that nothing stood between the enemy and his family.

Daniel wished his father, Eli, could just deal with the Nethog like he did last time. Daniel assumed that Eli, a mighty man of renown, could handle anything. That was true most of the time, but not today. Today it was Daniel's turn to defend the family. So Daniel rode and worried and wondered how he could possibly win.

* * *

Rog's cavalry corps rode up and down all the streets of the village located just inside the gates of Abel's Wall. They burned everything to the ground. Rog rode up to the center of the village, where a massive Flag of Heirs still flew majestically. Rog decided to rip it out and dismounted to do it. But no matter how hard he tried he could not budge it. He pushed and pulled but the flagpole with its five-colored flag still flew high up above him.

Rog's commanders, led by Grog and Magrog, gathered around him. Rog did not want to look weak in front of them so he remounted his carnotaur and ordered them to raise their banners. Two thousand riders unfurled orange and black flags adorned with their evil green symbol of a serpent. Then they rampaged toward the House of Esther and the end of the world.

Chapter 13
Jack's Faith

Jack woke up in bed with a cast on his slingshot arm. He sat up and saw his mom and dad. Behind them sat Sarah, soothing his sobbing sister Holly. Josh stood next to Jack's bed and announced he was no longer secretly jealous of Jack's pilgrimage. His dad suggested it was almost a miracle that Jack had survived the crash.

That got Jack thinking about miracles. He could have died at least three times: at the gold mine in Havilah, at the Steps of Sorrow, and just now. He was lucky to be alive. But was it luck, or something else? No, not something…Someone!

Jack watched their dad leave with a Blue Buccaneer. Then he noticed that his mother and Sarah were momentarily distracted by Holly's howling. Both Jack and Josh abruptly decided to follow their father. Geneva noticed them leave and was about to call them back when she collapsed in labor pain.

* * *

Daniel rode out across the fields to stop the enemy and save his family. Then he noticed a dinosaur galloping toward him. The wild-eyed beast was dragging Karl the Cainite behind it through the tall grass. The traitor had been betrayed!

Daniel dismounted, reached out, and grabbed the reins of Karl's wild-eyed dinosaur. After slowing the beast, Daniel quickly cut the Cainite free from his bonds. Then Daniel remounted his dinosaur and rode away. Karl just sat there in shock and said nothing.

* * *

Daniel rode hard toward the approaching horde. To his relief, their leader signaled his commanders to stop. Daniel could see that their leader was much amused at the sight of a single soldier standing in his way.

Daniel prayed silently and eased off his saddle with his staff in hand. He pointed his stick directly at their leader and said, "I'll fight you for Eli's Land. The loser leaves forever!"

"You want a fight?" laughed Rog. "Then face my revenge!" At Rog's command, Grogger, a ten-foot-tall mammoth monstrosity of a man, rode up to meet Daniel. He rode bareback, with no reins, on the biggest Tyrannosaurus rex Daniel had ever seen. The green-painted warrior held a massive club in each hand.

The T-rex roared at Daniel. They circled round and round as the Nethog chanted Grogger's name. Suddenly the T-rex lunged at Daniel with its jaws wide open. Daniel jammed his staff right into the dinosaur's mouth. The mighty dinosaur tried to snap the staff in half. But it only wedged it deeper into its jaws.

The T-rex jerked its head back and forth, but Daniel somehow clung to his staff inside the dinosaur's drooling jaws. Then Daniel saw that the T-rex had a loose tooth. He kicked it, hard! Daniel's big toe broke as the T-rex's tooth flew out and the T-rex howled in pain.

Daniel jumped clear of the T-Rex with staff in hand and landed on the ground. Grogger and

Daniel circled each other again. This time the T-rex kept its mouth shut as Grogger halfheartedly swung his clubs. The giant kept glancing at his injured pet.

Daniel noticed that Grogger was more worried about his T-rex than the fight. He pole-vaulted onto the head of the dinosaur. Grogger slammed his clubs down. But Daniel jumped off and Grogger pounded his T-rex senseless instead!

The unconscious dinosaur crashed to the ground causing Grogger to drop his clubs in surprise. Daniel took a hard swing at Grogger with his staff. But the giant ducked and decked Daniel instead. As Daniel flew backward he managed to thump Grogger's head. Both warriors collapsed.

When Grogger didn't get up at all, the Nethog slowly stopped cheering. Rog grabbed the staff from Daniel and walked over to Grogger. Then Rog poked the giant with it. The horde was silent. Rog had lost!

Grog and Magrog finally had the excuse they were looking for. They attacked their father. The horde hooted and hollered again. This was Nethog sport at its best.

In the chaos Daniel found himself scooped up by Karl. "Just keeping my options open," whispered

Karl with a grin as they turned and rode hard for the House of Esther.

Grog and Magrog's coup lasted until Rog overpowered them with Daniel's stick. Moments later they both lay on the ground, gasping for breath. Rog walked back to his carnotaur and tucked the staff into his saddle. He thought it would make a great souvenir. Grog and Magrog slowly got up and stumbled away as the Nethog jeered at them to go back home.

"Revenge!" shouted Rog as he held his crossbow high and mounted his mighty carnotaur. As the sun set the Nethog lit their torches and rode hard for the House of Esther.

Soon Rog saw Karl and Daniel fleeing in the far distance. He fired his crossbow and sent their dinosaur tumbling to the ground. Karl the Cainite never moved again. All his options were over.

* * *

Eli heard the deep sound of a thunderous boom behind him. He turned and looked up expecting to see his trumpeters sounding the alarm again from the very top of the House of Esther. But he saw something entirely unexpected instead. The Sword of Fire, far to the north at the gate to the Garden of Eden, had erupted! Now a bright line of crackling fire and lightning soared high across the night sky above him.

* * *

Draco saw many Blue Buccaneers and Purple Peacekeepers look up to the sky. Those that did look up dropped their weapons.

"Make them fight!" said Draco as he raced with his Red Thorn Rangers up the steps to Eli.

"The battle is over," said Eli, as George joined them.

"You're crazy!" said Draco, watching the raging horde get closer and closer.

Eli looked at his son sadly and said, "Look to the sky with the eyes of faith."

"Faith is for fools!" said Draco as he raced back down the steps with his Red Thorn Rangers.

* * *

Jack and Josh had to dodge past Draco and his Red Thorn Rangers to make it up the steps to their dad and Great-grandpa Eli. Then they saw the Nethog roaring toward them through the tall grasslands for the first time. They were monstrous, and moments away.

Jack thought about fighting or fleeing. But then Jack made a different decision. He decided to believe in God. He would believe, even if it meant his death moments from now or a life lived for centuries. Jack put his faith in the Lord and confessed his sins. He knelt in prayer and then stood up as a born-again creation.

Meanwhile, Josh stared up at the streak of fire racing across the night sky. He said, "Jack, check out that fire!"

"I don't need to see it now," said Jack. He somehow felt at peace with a blessed assurance. Both Eli and George smiled. Jack had finally begun his pilgrimage of faith.

* * *

Rog led the raging horde through the grasslands toward the House of Esther. Soon he would take Eli's Sword of Fire and live forever! He saw Daniel pinned and praying under the dead dinosaur. The supernaturally sinister, green-skinned giant general aimed his crossbow.

As Rog pulled the trigger, fire and lightning dropped from the sky and consumed nearly all of the Nethog in an instant. Their carnotaurs and crossbows were simply gone. Not a single blade of grass burned. Not a trace of smoke drifted into the night sky. Even the odor of volcanic ash was gone.

* * *

There were hugs and handshakes all around as Eli, George, Jack, Josh, and others burst into cheers. Suddenly a Purple Peacekeeper rushed up and told George that Geneva was in labor. George took off running toward the Birthing Chambers. But Jack and Josh just looked at each other and said, "Gross!"

Chapter 14
After the Fire

Mack found and followed Marco and Draco as they boarded a boat filled with Red Thorn Rangers in the harbor. They cast off and the warriors began rowing away. Moments later they all saw Daniel hobbling down the dock. He shouted that they had won the war.

Draco impulsively grabbed a spear and hurled it at Daniel. But Mack threw his boomerang just in time to knock the spear out of the sky. Then he reached up and caught his boomerang as it came back to him. That made Draco furious, until Marco stepped up, promising to punish the little traitor.

Marco grabbed Mack's boomerang and felt a twinge from the scratch on his sore shoulder. He happened to glance at the Mark of Cain on his own forearm. Then Marco saw Draco bullying his battle-weary rangers to make them row faster. That made him mad! He suddenly demanded that Draco make Mack a Red Thorn Ranger.

Marco's boldness enraged Draco, until the tyrant noticed everyone angrily staring at him. Draco slyly agreed to Marco's demand. Tensions on deck eased and Draco felt an inkling of respect for his firstborn son. Marco gave Mack back his boomerang and both of them felt a little more like the warriors they had always hoped to be.

* * *

Esther looked down in the moonlight at the Cainite boat fleeing the harbor. A silent tear slipped down her face as she thought of her son Draco. Eli rolled up, slowly and unsteadily stood, and hugged his wife. He did not say a word. After centuries of marriage, words were unnecessary.

* * *

Grogger woke up in the darkness. He sat up and felt a bump on his head. Then he gently rubbed the nose of the T-rex he had raised from birth. The beast woke up with a snort. It sniffed Grogger and didn't need the smell of ash to know not to eat him. Then they headed for home. Soon they caught up with Grog and Magrog, going the same way.

* * *

Mara, Melissa, and Delilah argued on and on about who got to eat one last raw frog leg. They were now safe in a hunter's camp, high up in the miserable mountains of the Lands of Noor.

Kaligu just smiled and smiled and made plans to sneak away to the Lands of Neer. After fleeing from Draco's city of Narl, Kaligu had met Simon. Simon had told him that, in Neer, there were no rules and all the food was free.

* * *

Jack jogged through the tall grass on the green plains of Eli's Land the next day. He wanted to pray at the spot where the Sword of Fire had wiped out the Nethog. He knew he was almost there because the tall grass up ahead had been flattened by the

Nethog's carnotaurs. Then Jack ran into something supernaturally sinister!

Rog, scarred and charred, slowly stood, holding Daniel's blackened staff. Jack fumbled with his slingshot and managed to painfully load a gold nugget. He was frantically aiming for the giant's forehead when he noticed Rog do something odd.

The giant simply dropped Daniel's staff. "You win this round, kid," grunted Rog, pulling off his roasted and toasted armor. Then Rog slowly sat back down in a sign of supernaturally subdued surrender.

* * *

Geneva cuddled her new baby girl. Labor had been long, but now it was over. Her husband slept in a chair next to her. She smiled at the thought of their new baby's name: Hope.

* * *

Kustodean pulled back a curtain on the stage of Seth's Cathedral for Eli and the surviving Council of Heirs later that week. They walked out as a sad and solitary trumpet played. Somber survivors had gathered together to grieve their many losses.

Eli shared from his heart. He challenged his children to seek the Lord. He reminded them that God was good and not the cause of evil. He looked forward to the day when the Messiah would rule and reign. A whirlwind of hard funerals honoring the fallen followed, including one for Karl the Cainite at Daniel's request.

* * *

Rick, Roger, and a few other surviving Green Guardsmen wandered through the wreckage of the city of Nitt. They were ready and willing to do whatever it took to survive and thrive. As a symbolic first step they replaced the apple tree on their coat of arms with a rhino.

* * *

Sarah rocked Holly to sleep in her cradle. Then she slumped down in a chair. She blamed herself for the death of her husband. After all, it had been her idea to flee to the Deep Drop.

"Anything happen while I was gone?" asked Ben, limping into the room.

Sarah jumped up and hugged her husband through her tears. "I…I thought you were dead."

"Let me just say the Deep Drop is really, really, deep," sighed Ben as he finally smiled.

* * *

Jack and his family walked in the grasslands outside of the House of Eve after a breakfast freely provided by Joe the Baker the next morning. A new puppy followed Jack. It was a belated birthday present from his grandparents. Hundreds of people were everywhere. They gathered in groups of prayer and praise to God.

Jack's dad carried Holly, who never seemed to cry when held by her father. Jack's mom carried Hope and wondered why she had come out here so soon after giving birth. But Deborah, Nicole, and Natalie were a big help. Natalie was quite pleased to note she had not been called a child by Nicole since breakfast.

Great-grandpa Eli and Great-grandma Esther walked hand in hand. The triplets, Bill, Bob, and Butch wrestled with each other, but in a fun and friendly way. Uncle Matt, his fortune lost but his faith found, walked with Kelli. Sam chased Josh in circles around Grandpa Daniel, who leaned on his cleaned-up staff and cheered.

The laughter of children mingled with the joy of their parents. Jack didn't feel like a kid and he didn't feel like an adult. He did feel saved, but it was more than just a feeling. A new day had dawned and that was enough…for now.

THE END

Epilogue

Og, Emperor of the Nethog, was quite upset when he finally heard the news…

People

Ben: A Captain in the Blue Buccaneers
Bill, Bob, & Butch: Jack's cousins
Daniel & Deborah: Jack's grandparents
Draco & Delilah: Mack's grandparents
Eli & Esther: Jack & Mack's great-grandparents
First Parents: Read the Book of Genesis ☺
George & Geneva: Jack's parents
Grog & Magrog: Rog's rebellious sons
Jack: A firstborn Sethite heir on a pilgrimage
Josh, Holly, Hope: Jack's siblings
Kaligu: Draco's arrogant doorkeeper
Karl: A mysterious Red Thorn Ranger
Kelli: Jack's spoiled cousin
Kustodean: Daniel's portly new butler
Mack: A firstborn Cainite heir on a quest
Marco & Mara: Mack's parents
Melissa: Mack's sister
Natalie & Nicole: Mack's friends
Nethog: Supernaturally sinister giants
Og: Emperor of the Nethog
Rick & Roger: Junior Green Guardsmen
Rog: General of the Nethog cavalry corps
Sarah: Jack's nanny and Ben's wife

Family Tree

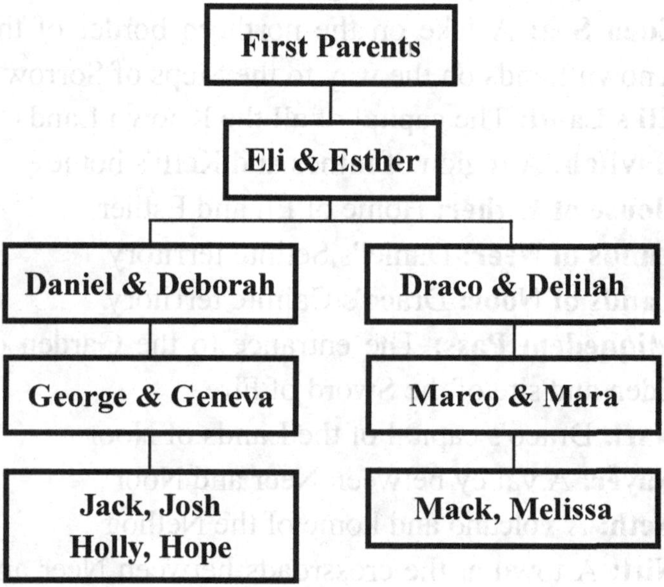
First Parents
Eli & Esther
Daniel & Deborah
Draco & Delilah
George & Geneva
Marco & Mara
Jack, Josh
Holly, Hope
Mack, Melissa

Places

Abel's Wall: A wall protecting Eli's Land
Adam's Way: A road connecting Neer and Noor
Bridge of Peace: A little-used bridge across the southern Nayer Valley connecting Neer and Noor
Deep Drop: A gorge carved by the Euphrates River marking the southern edge of Neer
Eden Sea: A lake on the northern border of the Known Lands on the way to the Steps of Sorrow
Eli's Land: The capital of all the Known Lands
Havilah: A region of mines and Kelli's home
House of Esther: Home of Eli and Esther
Lands of Neer: Daniel's Sethite territory
Lands of Noor: Draco's Cainite territory
Miqqedem Pass: The entrance to the Garden of Eden and site of the Sword of Fire
Narl: Draco's capital of the Lands of Noor
Nayer: A valley between Neer and Noor
Neth: A volcano and home of the Nethog
Nitt: A town at the crossroads between Neer and Noor and the home of the Green Guardsmen
Noll: Jack's home on the frontier of Neer
Noss: Daniel's capital city of the Lands of Neer
Steps of Sorrow: The way up to Miqqedem Pass

Postscript

Dear Reader,

You have reached the last page of my book. But the next page of your life has just begun! John 3:16 says:

> "For God so loved the world that He gave His one and only Son, that whoever believes in Him shall not perish but have eternal life."

The clock is ticking on your life and time flies! What will you decide? Will you suffer the Lord's "Sword of Fire" justice? Or will you accept the Lord's sacrificial love? God's love is the mercy and grace found on the cross of Jesus Christ and in His empty tomb. The choice is yours. Your eternity depends upon making the right decision.

Check out www.talesofeden.com and post a comment or ask a question about my book. My email is john@talesofeden.com. I would love to hear about your pilgrimage of faith!

- John R. Beck, 2019

Printed in the United States
By Bookmasters